FLOWERS*IN*WINTER

HART of ROCK and ROLL BOOK FIVE

MARY J. WILLIAMS

© 2017

ABOUT THE AUTHOR

Writing isn't easy. But I love every second. A blank screen isn't the enemy. It is the opportunity to create new friends and take them on amazing adventures and life-changing journeys. I feel blessed to spend my days weaving tales that are unique—because I made them.

Billionaires. Songwriters. Artists. Actors. Directors. Stuntmen. Football players. They fill the pages and become dear friends I hope you will want to revisit again and again.

Thank you for jumping into my books and coming along for the journey.

<u>*HOW TO GET IN TOUCH*</u>

Please visit me at these sites, sign up for my newsletter or leave a message.

http://www.maryjwilliams.net/

https://www.bookbub.com/authors/mary-j-williams

https://www.facebook.com/maryjwilliamsauthor/?ref=hl

https://twitter.com/maryjwilliams05

https://www.pinterest.com/maryj0675/

https://www.instagram.com/2015romance/

https://www.goodreads.com/author/show/5648619.Mary_J_Williams

MORE BOOKS BY MARY J. WILLIAMS

Harper Falls Series

If I Loved You

If Tomorrow Never Comes

If You Only Knew

If I Had You (Christmas in Harper Falls)

Hollywood Legends Series

Dreaming With a Broken Heart

Dreaming With My Eyes Wide Open

Dreaming Again

Dreaming of a White Christmas

(Caleb and Callie's story)

One Pass Away Series

After the Rain

After All These Years

After the Fire

Hart of Rock and Roll

Flowers on the Wall

Flowers and Cages

Flowers are Red

Flowers for Zoe

**One Strike Away**

For a Little While

For Another Day

For All We Know

For the First Time

WITH ONE MORE LOOK AT YOU

TABLE OF CONTENTS

CHAPTER ONE

HER NAME WAS Tula.

Born Petula Joyce Carson. When she was little, her family called her Petula Joyce. Later, simply Petula. However, on the day she began the second grade, she put her little, but determined foot down. She would only answer to Tula.

Why? All summer long, her cousin Bert—born a week earlier—but infinitely less mature—started calling her Petal in the most annoying, sing-song voice ever.

Ignore him, Tula's father counseled. *Bert will get tired of teasing you. He'll find someone else to torment.* She tried. Truly. But by the end of August, she'd had enough. Bert ended up with a fat lip, and he never called her Petal again.

And Petula became Tula.

The incident had become a Carson-clan legend. Tula tended to think as the years passed, the story had become blown out of proportion. Expanded with each telling for the entertainment of her large, raucous, loving, sometimes smothering, though always well-meaning family.

Tula wished the incident had been the beginning, not the end, of her rebellious ways. Oh, she had no problem standing up for others. She could, and would, fight when she witnessed injustice. Friends in need never hesitated to come to her. Without a second thought, she gladly did what she could to help.

For the life of her, Tula couldn't pinpoint the moment the feisty little girl turned into the stagnating woman. But she knew one thing. She had to change. Shake up her world before she found herself irrevocably bogged down in a job she didn't like, married to a decent but boring man, and pregnant long before she was ready.

Tula could feel the resentment build even though she was still free to choose. What would happen if she let herself fall into a pre-set life? What if she didn't put up a fight? Now. When she still had the chance. Would she stay silent until, at the age of forty, her head literally exploded? Or would she turn into a harpy who made the life of her unremarkable, yet kind husband a living hell? Not to mention her poor children.

Tula wiped her hands on her jeans. Other than the light from the computer screen, the room was dark as though she was afraid too much illumination would make her chicken out.

Now or never, she told herself. Tula took a breath. *Now.* She hit the send button and waited for an alarm to sound. Or her laptop to burst into flames. Instead, a message popped onto the screen.

Congratulations. We received your entry. The winner will be announced on September twenty-first. Good luck.

September twenty-first. Tula's birthday. Should she consider the date, three months away, to be an omen? Or a mere coincidence? The latter, she decided. The chance she would win was a long shot. However, even a chance was better than nothing. Right?

Tula felt a burst of excitement. Something had changed the second she hit send. If she won, she would grab the opportunity and run, literally, out of her small hometown.

If she lost? Tula laughed. *Actually* laughed. If she lost, the result had to be the same. She *had* to get out.

With a snap, Tula closed the laptop. Tonight, she'd planted a seed, and she was the only person she could count on to make certain the tiny kernel grew big, strong, and wonderful.

Tonight, was the beginning. Of what? Only time would tell. But one thing was certain. Tula Carson had finally learned how to dream.

CHAPTER TWO

"TIME'S UP, FLEET." Roni McKay took a pile of papers from her burgundy leather satchel. In her other hand, she held a flash drive. "You have to make a decision."

"*Have* to?" Fleet Sherman laughed at the very idea. He continued his set of bicep curls. "Do you know why I've worked my ass off day after day. Night after night? Why I've banked a shitload of money, power, and influence?"

"Because money, power, and influence are very good things?"

"Naturally."

Fleet flashed his manager one of his patented smiles. Over the years, Roni had grown immune to his charms—thank goodness. While he thrived on fawning fans, when he walked off stage and into his personal life, he wanted—needed—a hardnosed business associate. Someone who had his best interests at heart and wasn't afraid to knock him down a peg or two when necessary.

Roni McKay, barely five feet tall and maybe a hundred pounds soaking wet, was just such a person. Stark white hair worn in a short, no-nonsense cut, Fleet had never seen her dressed in anything but black. Roni had turned sixty last month, but she thought young, and she had the energy of a woman half her age.

More than his manager, Roni was his friend. He loved her. Respected her. But he never wanted her to lose sight of the facts. He paid her salary. He was in charge. He made the decisions. He, and nobody else.

The charming glint in Fleet's green-flecked hazel eyes sharpened.

"Every time my newest album skyrockets to number one? When my concerts sell out in ten minutes flat? I move further and further away from ever *having to* do a damn thing, Roni."

Roni sighed, her expression, if not her words, conveyed her current opinion of Fleet. His lips twitched, so tempted to break into a cocky grin. But for the sake of her blood pressure, he did something out of character. He restrained himself.

"*Write with Fleet?*" Roni prompted. "Remember?" When Fleet shrugged, Roni started to tap her foot—a sure sign her patience had started to crumble. "You approved the contest last December."

"Huh." Fleet searched his memory. "Remind me why?"

"Because, and I quote, *young songwriters need encouragement. They need a hand up. A place to grow their talents. All they hear is no. I want to be the one to tell one of them yes.*"

"Kind of sounds like me," Fleet nodded. "I'm a hell of a guy, aren't I?"

"One day soon you might consider adding a new room for your ever-expanding ego."

Again, Fleet tamped down his urge to smile. Muscles humming, Fleet returned the barbell to its designated place and wiped the sweat from his face. The upper floor of his Vermont country home was a state of the art fitness center. From a computerized rowing machine to a swimming pool. High tech all the way.

Expensive gadgets didn't make working out enjoyable—he hated exercise with a passion. However, like his voice, he depended on his body for his livelihood.

Genetically, Fleet was predisposed to chunky, if not downright fat. What his fans saw, what they expected, was a man who—thanks to daily self-inflicted torture sessions—didn't carry an extra ounce of flesh on his sleekly muscled six-foot-two-inch frame.

Fleet's fans didn't care that he would rather spend his time flat on his back, munching Cheetos and drinking beer while he binge-watched *Firefly* for the twentieth time. For their hard-earned money, they expected a rock star who didn't huff and puff his way around the stage.

Pride in his appearance was impetus enough to get Fleet's ass into the gym. The driving desire to stay on top was an extra push on days when vanity wasn't quite enough.

"Tell me what you need." Fleet dropped the attitude. He knew Roni's limit.

"The judges—handpicked by you—narrowed the field to ten. Here is a brief bio of each finalist." Roni handed Fleet the papers with the flash drive on top. "Plus the demos of their songs."

Fleet eyed the teal flash drive. His favorite color. Hardly a coincidence. Roni knew anything that appealed to him visually was more likely to keep his attention. Fleet didn't know if the characteristic—one that put him on the level of a three-year-old child—was a flaw or virtue. He had to give his manager props for creativity.

"Too bad you didn't download the songs onto an iPod." Maybe Roni didn't know him as well as she thought. "I could have listened to them while I ran."

"Here you go."

Her expression smug, Roni showed him a brand new iPod. Also in teal. Pre-loaded with contest entries, Fleet presumed.

With an upward tick of his eyebrow, Fleet zipped his hoodie to his neck. Bending, he switched out his shoes for the pair he used for his seven-mile-long cross-country treks.

"Well?" Roni asked.

Resigned to his defeat, Fleet held out his arm.

"Strap her on."

"CONGRATULATIONS. YOU WON."

Tula sank onto the faded chambray sofa. She kept a death grip on the phone in case the numbness in her legs spread north to her fingers.

"Say again?" she croaked out.

"My name is Roni McKay, Fleet Sherman's manager. I'm pleased to announce you are the lucky winner of the *Write with Fleet* contest." The woman laughed. "Though from Fleet's reaction to your song, luck had nothing to do with his choice."

For a second, Tula thought she might pass out. Until she remembered her brain needed oxygen and she pulled a deep breath into her air-deprived lungs.

"Are you sure you didn't make a mistake?"

"Are you Tula Joyce?"

"Yes." Tula had filled out the entry form with her first and middle names. She'd purposefully left off her last.

"And did you, Tula Joyce, enter the *Write with Fleet* contest?"

"I did. But—"

"No mistake. End of story. You're the winner."

Dreams were one thing, Tula realized. Reality was something else. She wasn't sure how to react beyond stunned. All she could think was, *happy birthday to me*.

8

"I don't know what to say." Tula laid her hand over her wildly beating heart, afraid the organ might burst from her chest at any second. "Thank you?"

"Don't thank me," Roni McKay said, her voice a bit gruff but friendly. "You did all the work. You and Fleet. Speaking of whom. He'd like to meet you before the press conference."

"Sure. Great. I— Wait." Tula swallowed. "Did you say press conference?"

"Naturally. You won a high-profile contest. You'll collaborate with one of the most respected and popular songwriters in the world. What did you think? We'd keep the news to ourselves?"

"But, I don't want my picture taken."

Had she whined, Tula wondered. The idea mortified her.

"Honey." Somehow, Roni managed to convey condescension and exasperation in one hefty sigh. "The whole point is publicity."

Tula wanted to cry. And scream. And stomp her feet. She wanted to regress back into a two-year-old who could get away with a temper tantrum. As an adult, expectations were different. If she threw her grandmother's glass vase across the room in frustration, she would have to clean up the mess. The contest had been an impetuous action. Now, she had to deal with the consequences.

"What if I don't want the publicity?"

Roni didn't answer immediately as if she needed time to digest Tula's question.

"You already agreed."

"I did?" Tula frowned. "When?"

"When you entered the contest. Didn't you read the rules and conditions?"

What Roni asked, but didn't come right out and say was, *didn't Tula read the fine print*? Tula wanted to shout back, *who the hell reads the fine print? I'll tell you who. Nobody. That's who.* Once more, she checked her baser instincts and remained calm. At least outwardly.

"For the sake of argument? What would happen if I refused?"

"As in no pictures or press conference?" Roni laughed as if the idea was preposterous. Unthinkable. "If you refuse to take part in the publicity campaign, Fleet will have to pick a different winner."

"Okay."

"Great. In two weeks, we'll fly you to New York and—"

"No," Tula interrupted. "I meant, okay, pick a different winner. Please thank Fleet. I'm flattered he thought so highly of my song."

"You can't be serious," Roni exploded. "Nobody ever says no to Fleet Sherman."

In the face of mass disappointment, Tula felt a burst of inexplicable pride as her offbeat sense of humor came to her

10

rescue. She was the first person to say no to the great Fleet Sherman? Yay! Break out the marching band.

"I didn't say no," Tula qualified.

"Then what—?"

"I said thanks, but no thanks."

"What's the freaking difference?" Roni asked.

"According to my mother, a *world* of difference," Tula said, perfectly aware how pompous she sounded. "Polite manners is what separates us from the animals. Goodbye, Ms. McKay. Give my congratulations to whomever came in second."

"Don't you dare hang up," Roni McKay warned. "Don't—"

Tula cut the woman off with a tap of her finger. With something between a sob and a whimper, she slid from the sofa to the floor. She'd been handed her dream by Fleet Sherman and promptly thrown his gift back in his face. What did that make her?

"A fool? A coward?" Tula chided herself.

No, she decided. Her problem was bigger than a yellow streak down her back. Much bigger.

Break out the straitjacket, folks. Petula Joyce Carson had plowed over the line from foolish to certifiably, undeniably, batshit crazy.

CHAPTER THREE

TULA TOSSED AND turned in her usually comfortable bed for over a week. With little sleep to show for her efforts. *Surprise, surprise.* Gnawing regret had a way of keeping her awake.

Then, around the time the first sliver of dawn's light peeked through her bedroom curtains, she would remember her mother's words.

"Nobody who is loved is ever without hope. And you, my darling Tula, are well and truly loved."

Like a comforting hug, the reminder would relax Tula's mind and body, and allow her to drift to sleep for a few hours.

On day nine, showered, dressed, and a bit bleary eyed, Tula stood in her small, barely serviceable kitchen. As she waited for a fresh pot of strong coffee to brew, she faced another morning of doubt and self-recriminations.

Love and hope. Why, Tula asked herself as she took a mug from the cupboard, had she allowed one emotion to set up a huge, seemingly insurmountable, roadblock for the other? Why didn't she have the courage to embrace her family's love? And *hope* they would understand.

As Tula leaned against the counter, coffee in hand, her thoughts wandered. Though she'd lived here since her junior year of college, through graduate school, and while she worked on her Ph.D. in education, the apartment wasn't home. She'd added her own touches to make the four rooms comfortable, but in the end, they were a place to live. Somewhere to hang her clothes, and rest her head when she wasn't in class or at work.

Home had always been where Tula grew up. Three hundred miles north. On her family's farm just outside of South Ridge, Alabama. The memories were so strong at times, she swore she could smell the new-mown hay. And taste her mother's cooking. And hear the voices of her five brothers and sisters. Loud voices. The halls of the Carson home were never silent.

Money was tight in those days. But their stomachs were always full. As a child, Tula experienced the usual growing pains. She fought with her siblings. Argued with her parents. But with the eyes of an adult, she could see how lucky she'd been.

Joy. Love. Happiness. And now, guilt.

We're so proud, Tula, had become her family's standard greeting. Hello was too mundane for the Carson clan. *We're so proud.* Followed by a litany of her accomplishments. *College. Graduate school. Soon, a Ph.D. Next year, you'll be back in South Ridge where you belong. At the local high school. A full-fledged teacher.*

Tula slammed the mug onto the counter. Naturally, coffee splashed onto her freshly laundered blouse. With a hefty, fatalistic sigh, she removed the stained garment, walked to the bathroom, and filled the sink with cool water.

As much as I love you and the memories, I don't belong in South Ridge, she wanted to tell her family. Maybe one day. But not now. *And, I don't want to be a teacher*.

In her mind, Tula had blurted out the shameful confession a thousand times. And in her mind, her family always understood. They loved her. Wanted her to be happy.

However, when the moment came, she could never get the words past the lump in her throat. The time was never right, she told herself. But the truth? She was a coward. About everything.

Tula couldn't tell her family what she wanted. And when the chance to have her heart's desire arrived on a silver platter? Did she embrace her dream? Did she say the hell with what anybody else thought? Nope. Not only did she refuse the precious opportunity, she practically threw the gift back into the giver's face.

At least she hadn't forgotten to say thank you, Tula thought with a humorless snort.

Tula raised her gaze from where a steady stream of water swirled around her coffee-covered blouse to the mirror, blind to the lovely young woman other people saw. Her delicate, even features favored the Gallic side of her mother's family. High cheekbones. Oval face. Lips that more often than not tended to curve upward, not down. A slender neck led to an equally slender, yet strong, body.

No, when Tula looked at herself, she didn't see a beautiful, vibrant young woman, her future filled with endless possibilities. Her dark gaze was too filled with recriminations to look past today and the bags under her eyes.

Sick of herself and her endless loop of repetitious thoughts, Tula slipped her arms into a clean shirt from her closet. She'd planned on a nice, quiet morning alone. She might work on a new song.

Tula almost chuckled. *Almost.* Music both kept her awake at night *and* calmed her. The irony wasn't lost on her.

When a loud knock broke her reverie, Tula said a silent prayer. Tired of her own company, she couldn't get to the door fast enough. She didn't care if every Bible-thumping soul saver in the state was lined up around the block. If they helped her climb out of her own head for a little while, she would welcome each and every one with open arms.

The distance across the living room wasn't far. A few long strides and Tula threw open the door. Instead of two or three neatly dressed godly young men, she found one man. And by the look of him, he wasn't there to spread the Lord's word.

15

Thumbs hooked through the belt loops of a pair of worn jeans, one hip was slightly cocked in her direction. The faded blue t-shirt under a brown leather bomber jacket clung to his muscled torso. Scuffed boots on his feet. A boyish half smile on his lips and a twinkle in his gold-flecked eyes.

Not exactly the devil. But every inch of him screamed sin.

"Tula Joyce?" He said her name with the slightest hint of a lilting Irish brogue. "I'm—"

"I know who you are."

If Tula had lived under a rock for the last ten years, she still would have recognized Fleet Sherman. He was *that* famous. Which made his appearance on her doorstep a major shock to her already wobbly constitution.

"I'll introduce myself, nonetheless. Since you're such a stickler for good manners." He flashed a pair of straight, white teeth and held out his hand. "Fleet Sherman."

Heat colored Tula's cheeks at his *good manners* crack. He delivered the words with seeming good humor, but the phone call with his manager was too fresh in her mind for her to return his smile. If the floor had opened and sucked her in, she would have cheered.

Since the chance Tula would spontaneously disappear was slim to none, she took Fleet's hand—and pulled him into her apartment before her neighbor Mrs. Roland got a gander at Tula's famous

16

visitor. A born gossip, she carried a cordless handset in the pocket of her housecoat for just such occasions. In a flash, the news would be all over town.

"For a second, I didn't think you planned to invite me in. Though *invite* is a bit of a misnomer," Fleet chuckled.

"Why are you here, Mr. Sherman?" Tula demanded as she shut the door with a decisive click.

"Why do you think? Ms. *Carson?*"

"If I knew, I wouldn't have asked. I told your manager…"

Carson? Tula barely swallowed a groan. *Well, crap.* Forget a hole in the floor. She was already neck deep and sinking fast.

"You know who I am?" Or rather, Fleet found out who her brother was. Tula had a famous last name. *She* was nobody. "How?"

Fleet shrugged, his expression amused. "Twenty-first-century technology. Don't ask me the details. But my team did a thorough background check on every person who entered the contest. You included."

"Without my permission? How dare *your team* intrude on my privacy?"

Tula huffed and puffed, ready to spew her displeasure. Without a word, Fleet raised an eyebrow. She groaned. With one pointed look, he had effectively burst her bubble of outrage.

"I should have read the fine print," Tula groaned.

Fleet ran a hand through his artfully disheveled dark-blond hair. "Aye. The fine print will get you every time."

Had she seen a flash of sympathy in his hazel eyes? The moment passed so quickly—a blink—Tula couldn't be sure. Not that she cared. Fleet Sherman only had one thing she wanted. And since she'd already turned him down...

"Why *are* you here, Mr. Sherman?" Tula asked again.

"Would you mind if I sat down?" Fleet didn't wait for an invitation. With a sigh, he took a seat on her old, faded sofa, stretched out his long legs, crossing them at the ankles. "Long trip after a long night. Did you know your little college town doesn't have a decent airport? I had to drive all the way from Birmingham."

"Must have been quite a strain."

By the look he shot her, Tula could tell the sarcasm in her tone wasn't lost on Fleet. He simply chose not to comment.

"Water would be fantastic. Thank you."

Tula's gaze narrowed. Had Fleet just made another dig about her manners? Or lack thereof? His demeanor was so laidback, she couldn't tell. Was *Mr. Rock God* a passive aggressive asshole? Or was she overly sensitive? In her current state of mind, Tula preferred to think the fault lay with her uninvited guest.

"Mr. Sherman—"

"Please. Call me Fleet. And before you get me that water? Your shirt is a bit," Fleet cleared his throat. "Undone."

"What?" Tula looked down. In her haste to open the front door, she'd only fastened the bottom button. She scrambled to finish the job, more angry than embarrassed. "Why didn't you say something sooner?"

Fleet rolled to his feet, walked to the kitchen, and helped himself to a bottle of water from the refrigerator.

"I've had women flash more than their bras at me." With an unconcerned shrug, he unscrewed the lid, taking a sip. "I didn't want to comment until I was sure of your intentions. One way or the other."

"My intentions?" Tula rolled her eyes. Of all the egotistical jerks. "You aren't as irresistible as you think, *Mr. Sherman.*"

"What *I* think isn't the point," Fleet pointed out. "The thousands of fans who throw themselves at me daily tell the tale. *Ms. Carson.*"

A dozen responses popped into Tula's head. All designed to knock Fleet Sherman and his overblown opinion of himself down a few notches. Luckily, before she blasted him, she noticed the way Fleet's lips twitched as he took another drink of water.

"You're pulling my leg, aren't you?" Tula accused him. As the youngest of six, she'd endured her share of teasing and recognized the signs.

"Maybe. Just a little," Fleet conceded. "When you dragged me into your apartment, your motives seemed more frazzled than flirtatious. So I used what I had at my disposal to help you settle your thoughts."

"What you had at your disposal? As in your bloated ego?"

Again, Fleet shrugged his grin in full view.

"You say bloated, I say pleasantly plump."

Tula would have sworn she wasn't ready to let go of her somber mood. When she'd answered the door, her thoughts had been in a dark place, and the light seemed far, far away. Yet within minutes, Fleet Sherman had pulled off the impossible. He'd made her feel like laughing.

"Go on," Fleet urged as if he could read her thoughts. "My dear mother always says a good laugh and a long sleep are the best cures for anything. Since I traveled quite a distance to see you? Do me a favor. Laugh now. Sleep later."

Certain she had to be in the middle of an absurd dream, Tula did as Fleet asked. She laughed. And, she had to admit, felt better.

"Such a lovely sound," Fleet declared with a bemused tone.

Something sparked in Fleet's hazel eyes. The emotion came and went too quickly for Tula to identify. Gaze shuttered, Fleet deposited the empty water bottle in the trash.

"Would you like something else?" Tula inquired. "My sister sent me a batch of oatmeal cranberry cookies."

"I wish I could." With a look of regret at the nearby cookie jar, Fleet patted his flat stomach. "If I have one, I'll have six. I have a bit of a sweet tooth."

"If you change your mind, help yourself."

One second Tula and one of the most famous men on Earth were sparring over why he was there and her unbuttoned blouse. The next, he made her laugh, and she offered him cookies. Talk about surreal.

"Publicity. What's your hang up?"

Tula blinked. In five succinct words, Fleet's demeanor morphed from playful to all business. Honestly, the man made her head spin.

"Not a hang up. Exactly." Tula kept her response measured.

"Is your brother the problem?"

"What do you mean?" Tula held her breath, unsure if Fleet had figured out her motivation.

"Smith doesn't like to share the spotlight?" Fleet nodded as if he'd hit on the answer. "Don't get me wrong. I like to work solo. However, if I had a sister with half your talent, I'd do everything in my power to lift her up. Not shove her into the shadows."

Tula's spine stiffened. Fleet could shoot arrows her way all he liked. But nobody was allowed to insult a member of her family.

"My brother is the most generous person in the world."

"Generous?" Fleet scoffed. He looked around the tiny apartment. "We have a different definition of the word."

"Smith offered to pay for my education. And my living expenses." Smith had tried. And tried. And tried again to get Tula to change her mind. In fact, he'd tried again only a few days ago. "I make my own way."

"Admirable."

Arms crossed, her stance combative, Tula lifted her chin as if to say, take your best swing.

"Smith isn't stingy with his money. The dark-blue car in the parking lot was a gift from him on my birthday before last. Don't turn up your nose. Originally, he bought me a flashy little foreign number. I made him exchange the Ferrari for a Ford."

"I concede defeat." Fleet held up his hands in surrender. "Smith Carson is a saint."

"Hardly." Smith would have rolled on the floor with laughter at the thought. And Tula would have been right beside him. "He's my brother. And I love him. End of story."

"Except you didn't answer my question."

"Didn't I?" Tula, wide eyed, gave Fleet a puzzled frown.

"The contest?" Fleet reminded Tula with admirable patience. "If Smith isn't the problem, why did you turn down the win?"

The truth sounded lame, even to Tula. *I don't want to disappoint my family*, made her sound like a whiny little twit.

Which, she was afraid, wasn't far from the truth. Before she could think of a plausible lie, Fleet shot another question at her.

"Why did you enter in the first place?"

Tula swallowed. "I… Well…"

Fleet took a step toward her. And another. Small room. Long-legged man. His third step brought him so close, Tula could see the exact moment the flecks in his eyes turned from gold to green.

"Fascinating," she whispered.

"I agree," Fleet nodded. "Your motives fascinate me."

Tula felt an unexpected wave of disappointment. She had Fleet's eyes on her mind. All Fleet could think about was music. What had she expected? Men didn't lose their heads over her. Momentarily or otherwise. She was the girl next door. The buddy. The little sister.

Tula Carson wasn't the type to inspire unbridled desire in a man like Fleet Sherman.

Whoa. Tula put on the brakes, angry at herself because she never measured her worth by the approval in a man's gaze. And pissed off at Fleet for—inadvertently or not—flirting the thoughts into her head.

With a hard shove, Tula pushed Fleet away.

"I entered to see if my song was good enough," Tula said, satisfied with her answer.

"Your song was better than good enough, Tula. If you agree, I'd like to make *Crazy Day* my next single."

"Your next single?" Tula was sure she must have misunderstood. "Don't you want to make some changes? Rewrites? Some tweaks?"

Don't you want to have your head examined to see if you've lost your mind?

"Never doubt your work. Nothing is perfect. Believe me, I know," Fleet chuckled. "At some point, you have to let go. Worse than a bad song is an overworked one. You have a fresh sound, Tula. A strong voice."

"Really?"

Tula's *strong voice* sounded more like a breathless little girl. And she couldn't have cared less. Fleet Sherman wanted to record her song. *Holy crap.*

"Really," Fleet assured her.

"What about the contest?" Tula's stomach sank. *Damn rollercoaster emotions.* "I haven't changed my mind about the publicity."

"Women," Fleet sighed. "I handed you emeralds. Are you happy? Nope. *You* want to know where I hid the diamonds."

"You're sexist."

Disappointment didn't begin to describe Tula's reaction. She had started to put Fleet on a pedestal—a mistake under any circumstances. She didn't know whether to thank him for jolting her to her senses. Or kick him in the nuts for women worldwide.

If his slow smile was any indication, Fleet wasn't the least bit offended by Tula's accusation.

"Show me a man who swears up and down he isn't a bit sexist, and I'll show you a bald-faced liar." Fleet ran a hand over the cookie jar, shook his head, and moved on. "To my credit? I would have made a similar crack if you were a man."

"Equal opportunity sexism?" Tula asked, hands on hips.

"Exactly." With a sigh, Fleet sprawled onto the sofa. "Something besides emeralds and diamonds. A manlier metaphor."

Tula didn't know what to think. Fleet had just doubled down on his original sexist remark. He wasn't the least bit shy to share his less than PC opinions.

"Don't worry." Fleet stretched his arms over his head. "My sexism isn't rampant. A mild case, at best. Or do I mean worst?"

"Definitely worst."

"Sounds right," he nodded with a yawn. "Believe me. After we've worked together for a while, you'll find I'm a decent guy. But a bastard taskmaster."

To make certain she'd heard correctly, Tula closed her eyes and ran Fleet's last words through her mind. When she hit the good part, her eyes popped open.

"Work together? As in work? Together? You and me? Together?"

Fleet proved he wasn't a jerk. A good sign in Tula's estimation. He could have laughed at her reaction. Ridiculed her quick turnaround from enraged feminism to wide-eyed excitement. Instead, he took her by the arm. Sat her on the sofa. Brought her a bottle of water. And waited patiently for her to regain her composure.

Tula rebounded quickly. As her thoughts settled and her heartbeat returned to something close to normal, she looked at Fleet. Really looked at him. Beyond his handsome face and superstar status. And what she saw made her lips curve upward.

"You, Fleet Sherman, are a kind man."

Fleet winced. "Don't tell anybody. I have a reputation to maintain."

When Fleet winked, Tula's stomach did a slow roll. *Oh, boy*, she thought. She couldn't let herself fall under his charm. Not now. Not ever. She would be a fool to pine, even a little, over the notorious womanizer. An unrequited crush would be disastrous. To her ego. Her peace of mind. And especially to their working relationship.

Holy crap. Fleet Sherman wanted to work with her.

"I don't know if I should laugh or cry."

"Laugh. Please. I'm a washout when a woman cries. And in case you want to throw down the sexist gauntlet again? I'm even worse when a *man* cries."

Tula laughed. The kind of feel-good laugh that came from deep inside and spread through her body.

"Better. Now, about your song." Suddenly all business, Fleet took off his jacket. "The second verse needs a few tweaks."

"I thought you said *Crazy Day* didn't need work."

"You needed an ego boost. I said no song is perfect. Remember? Besides, I don't consider a few tweaks work." Frowning, Fleet looked around. "Paper. And something to write with. Preferably a pencil. Damn. I left my guitar in the rental car."

Before he could remove the keys from his pocket, Tula took Fleet's jacket.

"You can use mine," she said as she opened the hall closet. She hung his jacket next to her fleece-lined winter coat. Behind her winter boots, away from prying eyes, she found her guitar. "Unless you need your own. My brother swears the music sounds wrong on someone else's instrument."

Fleet snorted. "Smith Carson is a—"

"Careful," Tula warned. "I know I don't have any room to negotiate. However, unless you have something good to say, Smith is off limits."

"I like your brother." Tula gave him a skeptical look and Fleet shrugged. "I have no problem with him beyond a professional rivalry. And the curvy redhead he stole from me a few years back."

Tula didn't doubt her brother's prowess. Before he fell head over heels for Zoe Hart, Smith had a reputation to rival Fleet Sherman's. Exactly why she was surprised Fleet confessed his defeat.

"The curvy redhead? Was she the love of your life?" Tula asked, tongue firmly planted in her cheek. "Did Smith's superior romantic skills leave your heart irrevocably broken?"

"No, smartass." Fleet took her guitar. Head bent, he strummed the strings while he adjusted the pitch. "My heart was fine. As for my balls?"

"Blue?"

Fleet snorted. "You have a sense of humor. Thank the Lord."

Tula wasn't offended. She was reserved around people she didn't know. However, around her family and a few close friends, she was known for her ever-growing arsenal of dirty jokes.

"There once was a man from Nantucket..." she began.

"Been there, heard that," Fleet said with a dismissive shake of his head.

"I can guarantee you've never heard my version." Tula was certain because she'd written the limerick herself.

"Okay. Surprise me."

Tula shook her head as she set a stack of paper, six pencils, and a sharpener on the coffee table.

"My limericks are pretty dirty. I'll have to know you a lot better before I go there."

"Fair enough," Fleet chuckled. "Give me a timeline. A week? Two? A month?"

"Are we going to work together for a month?" The idea boggled Tula's mind.

"Longer. If we click." Satisfied with the sound, Fleet handed Tula the guitar. "I have writing partners I've worked with for years. I can be in Munich and still hammer out the kinks in a song with a guy in Los Angeles. Thank you, modern *Skype* and *FaceTime*."

"Will we?" Tula asked. "Click, I mean?"

"Only one way to find out. Play."

Before Tula could pluck a note, Fleet held up a hand.

"Stop. I'm done."

Had she screwed up already? Mouth agape, Tula watched Fleet stand. She wondered how he would react if she threw her arms around his legs and begged him not to go. She would gladly humble herself if she thought she might change his mind.

Fleet saved her the humiliation when he didn't head out the front door but instead, detoured to the kitchen.

"My willpower is low at the best of times," he sighed, lifting the lid from the cookie jar. "I can't hold out a second longer."

Bemused, and amused, Tula watched as Fleet waved the jar under his nose. Eyes closed, he inhaled deeply and smiled.

"Near heaven." The Irish in his voice deepened. Fleet took a cookie, bit down, and sighed. "Heaven proper."

"If you wanted a cookie so much, why did you wait?"

"Because along with lousy willpower, I'm, at heart, a glutton." Fleet loaded his hand with five cookies. Then six. He finally gave up and grabbed the jar. "I swear the fifth deadly sin was written with me in mind."

Damn the man, Tula thought. Fleet had the winning smile of a little boy packed in the body of a very grown up, *very* sexy man. A dangerous combination.

"Would you like a glass of milk?"

On his second cookie, Flint set the jar on the coffee table.

"I'd kill for a cup of tea. If you don't mind."

"No problem. Tea sounds good. Are you going to share?" Tula nodded toward the cookies.

"Depends. How many are you talking about?"

Laughing, Tula turned on the electric kettle. Fleet *was* a glutton. And funny. And smart. And absolutely adorable. All traits she could resist. But when he smiled at her with a twinkle in his sometimes green, sometimes gold-flecked eyes as though she was the only woman in the world?

Tula let out a long, heartfelt sigh. She was too smart. Too focused on her future to fall in love with anybody. Especially a lady's man like Fleet Sherman who was only out for a good time. However, if she wasn't extremely careful and vigilant, she could *easily* tip into lust.

CHAPTER FOUR

RESTED AND REJUVENATED after a long trip home, an extra-long workout as punishment for the dozen oatmeal cranberry cookies he'd scarfed down the day before, and a steam-heavy shower designed to loosen even the tightest muscles, Fleet listened to the finished song with fresh ears.

Yesterday? *Crazy Day* sounded like a hit. One day and a marathon writing session later? Tula Carson's *slightly* tweaked song sounded even better. Fleet wanted to record the track as soon as possible. Since he had a studio in his home and his favorite musicians on speed dial, Fleet didn't see time as a problem.

Fleet handed a cup of coffee to Roni McKay. With a sigh, he took a sip of his hot water and lemon juice. A little self-imposed deprivation would get his healthy regimen back on track. Not that he had a single regret. If a day spent laughing, singing with Tula while they gorged on music, cookies, *and* pizza meant he had to watch his calories with extra, extra care, he would take the trade-off six days a week and twice on Sunday.

"You should have told me where you were going. And what you planned to do when you arrived."

With a sigh, Fleet removed his noise-canceling earphones. The song—no matter how good—couldn't compete with Roni when she was in full-out scold mode.

"What would you have said if I told you I wanted to meet with Tula Carson on her own turf?"

"Don't go." Roni added a large dollop of cream to her coffee, followed by three heaping spoonfuls of sugar. "But if you do, don't make a commitment until you have everything in a contract, signed and notarized."

"And half the fun flies right out the window."

"Part of my job is to remind you that business comes before fun."

"My business is music. Music is fun. A fact I'd started to forget. Thanks to Tula Carson, I remembered. See?" Fleet pointed to his relaxed features. "In case you've forgotten, this is what happy looks like."

Roni took a chocolate muffin from the box of a dozen she'd purchased from Fleet's favorite bakery. Cursed with a sluggish metabolism, most days, he accepted Roni's ability to eat anything and never gain an ounce with a shrug. Today, he didn't feel as gracious. Especially since with every savored bit, she practically shoved the inequity of their situation in his face.

"I hate to burst your bubble."

"No, you don't."

"Yes, I do." Roni took another bite of muffin and chewed slowly. "You spent all day with Tula Carson?"

"I did."

"Writing?"

"No. We took one look at each other and started screwing like rabbits."

Fleet knew the second he met her—in spite of the inadvertently unbuttoned blouse—Tula wasn't the *fall in bed with a stranger* type. She was beautiful. And sexy as hell in a subtle, sneak up on him unexpectedly, kind of way.

"Of course not." Roni's sharp gaze narrowed. "Unless... From her picture, she didn't seem like your type. Too wholesome."

The memory of Tula's tale about her dirty limerick, and the depth of her songwriting, made Fleet smile. Sweet and spicy. The old adage, *never judge a book by its cover*, was a perfect fit for Tula Carson.

"Fleet..."

Fleet recognized the warning tone in Roni's voice. An excellent manager, she tried her best to rein in his baser instincts—to mixed results. An even better friend, she often reminded him that he wasn't his father's son. He wasn't a drunken charmer who used women then tossed them aside without a second thought.

Fleet could be careless. But he was never deliberately cruel.

"Tula and I worked. Period. No hanky-panky."

34

"Thank goodness for small blessings. Which brings me back to my original thought. You only have her word she won't hawk the song—and the improvements you made—to another artist. Her brother, for example." Roni raised an eyebrow. "I bet Smith Carson would love to record something written by you and not have to pay you a dime for your trouble."

"The song belongs exclusively to Tula. All I did was smooth out a couple of rough edges—with her help."

"Wait. You aren't getting a writing credit?"

Roni looked so appalled, as if she might pass out, Fleet tried his best not to grin. Potential medical emergencies were no laughing matter.

"Breathe, Roni. When I produce *and* record *Crazy Day*, the money will roll in. The song is a chart topper. Guaranteed."

"Unless Tula Carson screws you over. Rule one. Handshakes are cute. But get the agreement in writing."

"If Tula Carson breaks our verbal agreement, she isn't the woman I think she is." And Fleet would be disappointed. More than he wanted to admit. "I'll have wasted an afternoon. Nothing else."

Fleet didn't mention the three new songs he and Tula had completed after they worked on *Crazy Day*. He didn't want Roni to have a stroke.

"Your faith in human nature never fails to amaze me."

35

"Bollocks. My faith begins and ends with me." He raised his mug to Roni. "You taught me well."

"Good boy," Roni said like a proud parent. Which, in many ways, she was. "I hope your assessment of Tula Carson's character pans out. In the meantime, I had a contract drawn up and messengered to her. I hope she signs."

Blind faith was for fools. But Fleet was as certain about Tula as he could be. And since he trusted his gut, he knew she wouldn't disappoint him.

"Believe me, Tula will sign. And by Thanksgiving, we'll have a number one song."

"Thanksgiving is only two months away," Roni reminded him.

Fleet removed the headphones from his iPod and cranked up the volume. As the acoustic version of Crazy Day filled the room, he felt a familiar feeling zip through him. He looked at Roni, watched as a smile lifted her lips and her fingers tapped out the beat on the kitchen counter.

"Number one, baby." Fleet made a few perfectly synced dance moves. "Guaranteed."

CHAPTER FIVE

TWO MONTHS LATER

"YOU LOOK TIRED." Zoe Hart handed Tula a large platter from the china cabinet.

Tula set the family heirloom on the lace tablecloth next to the good silver, forks, knives, spoons, etc., and other dishes only brought out on special occasions. The scrumptious smells of her mother's traditional Thanksgiving meal surrounded Tula like a warm, welcome hug. Like every holiday she could remember, the house fairly burst at the seams with family and friends.

"I have to present my dissertation at the beginning of the year. Between the paper, and classes, and work, I'm a little frayed around the edges."

Not to mention the time Tula spent Skyping with Fleet. Because his schedule was as crazy as hers, they had to connect at odd hours. Last night, she didn't get to sleep until after four in the morning. But Tula loved every creative second. Besides, she was a young, healthy woman doing what she loved. She could sleep when she was dead. Or in February.

As Tula laughed, she felt an old, unwanted nemesis creep into the room. Guilt. For the first time since she had started college, money *wasn't* an issue. However, she couldn't tell Zoe why she didn't need a loan. Or could she.

Tula needed advice. And her future sister-in-law would have been the perfect sounding board. The gorgeous blonde hadn't been the easiest person to get to know, but slowly, as Zoe dropped her guard, she and Tula had become good friends.

Unfortunately, Tula didn't know if she wanted to put Zoe in the position where she had to keep a secret from the man she loved. Or, if she would even consider doing so.

Zoe groaned. "I'm sorry. I hate when someone says that to me. Feels like a backhanded way of telling me I look like crap. Which you don't, by the way."

"Thanks," Tula chuckled.

"I know money is a sore subject," Zoe began tentatively. "And I completely understand why you won't let Smith help. But I could float you a loan. No interest. You wouldn't have to pay me back for say, the next sixty or seventy years?"

"Question?" Rather than deal with the money issue, Tula focused on a safer subject. Zoe's sometimes unnerving perfection. "Just to make me and the rest of us mere mortals feel better? Name one time you looked like crap?"

"I don't roll out of bed looking like this." With a slow, self-aware smile, Zoe gave her long, honey-colored hair a playful flip. "Ask Smith."

Tula knew exactly what her brother would say. To him, Zoe always looked beautiful. And no matter how Zoe demurred, Tula tended to believe him. Whatever the time of day. Morning, noon, or night. After she played lead guitar in front of a packed stadium—more often than not dressed in spiked heels and leather—Zoe Hart somehow managed to look like she'd just stepped off the cover of a fashion magazine.

If Tula didn't love the woman like a sister, she would gleefully hate Zoe's guts.

"About Smith." Her mind made up, Tula lowered her voice to a conspiratorial whisper. "Can I tell you a major, my brother can't know, secret?"

Zoe turned serious.

"Are you in trouble?"

"No," Tula assured her. "And the secret is mine and mine alone. I wouldn't ask you to keep something from Smith if he were involved."

"If you or someone Smith cares about is involved, he's involved. However," Zoe said when Tula's shoulders drooped in defeat. "I understand your point. I won't tell Smith. Unless I have to."

Chances were good Zoe wouldn't have to keep quiet for long. Fleet Sherman's recording of *Crazy Day* had debuted on the *Billboard Hot 100* last week. With a bullet. He seemed to think the song would hit number one any day. She'd almost screamed her apartment walls down the first time she heard the song on the radio. And her first thought had been to call her parents to share her excitement. Instead, she danced around like a fool. Alone.

"Would somebody please turn off that song?" Smith yelled from the porch.

Tula felt a thrill she was certain would never grow old when she realized the song blasting from the living room was hers.

"I like *Crazy Day*." Nellie Carson walked from the kitchen, the apron she wore surprisingly stain-free after a day cooking. "The beat's contagious. And the words hopeful."

"I agree." Zoe's brother, Ryder Hart, swung a spry and willing Nellie into a jaunty two-step. On the way past the radio, he paused to turn up the volume. "Your son's problem isn't the song. Smith doesn't like the fact that Fleet Sherman passed him on the charts."

"*Pleasure Palace* was number one for a month." Smith sent a wink Zoe's way. "I don't see the Ryder Hart Band in the top ten."

"Check the list in January after our new album drops, pretty boy."

The mild insult rolled off Smith's back like water off a duck.

"Look in the mirror, Hart," he chided. "Your hair is almost as long as your sisters."

"My wife likes my hair, don't you, beautiful?"

Quinn Abernathy stopped taking pictures long enough to blow Ryder a kiss.

"I like you any way I can have you," she told him.

Now was the perfect time to confess all to her family, Tula knew. But she needed someone to practice on. As the good-natured ribbing continued, she saw her chance. She pulled a startled Zoe from the room and up the back stairs.

"Slow down," Zoe complained, though she let Tula maneuver her down the hall. "We have a concert on Sunday and two hours on stage with a sprained ankle doesn't sound like my idea of a good time."

Tula closed the door to her childhood bedroom and began to pace. Zoe, for all her grousing, calmly took a seat on the lace comforter and crossed her long legs, not a hair out of place.

"I need to tell somebody, or I'll pop." Tula made a sound as close to an explosion as she could manage. "Literally. Boom."

"You're pregnant."

"What?" The rug under Tula's feet slid several feet on the hardwood floor as she did her best to come to a screeching halt. "Are you out of your mind?"

"I tried to put myself in your shoes and the only scenario I can think of that would make me as frazzled would be a baby on the way."

"I'm not pregnant. Sheesh. I'm not even... I mean I have in the past... But not right now. You know?"

"Okay." Zoe nodded. "We've established that at one time, you were sexually active. You aren't at the moment. Which, short of an act of God, eliminates the old bun in the oven problem. Do you need a drum roll, or are you ready spill your guts?"

Tula took a deep breath. Swallowed. And spilled.

"I wrote *Crazy Day*."

Tula waited for her house of lies to crash down around her. Then she remembered. Zoe hadn't been family for long. The lies weren't as impactful. As meaningful. Still, Tula expected some reaction beyond a blank stare.

"Well?" Tula tossed her hands in the air. "Say something."

"If you gave me a thousand guesses, I would have missed by a mile. Every time."

"Because I'm boring? Untalented?"

"I know for a fact you're belly-laugh funny," Zoe said, her gaze direct. Her tone emphatic. "As for talent? You're a Carson. Music is in your blood. However, I thought Smith was the only member of your family who wanted to perform professionally."

"I don't want to perform." The idea made Tula shudder. As proud as she was of her brother, she couldn't understand how he walked onto a stage in front of one person, let alone tens of thousands. "All I want to do is compose music. And write the perfect words to match."

"Congratulations. Mission accomplished." Zoe wasn't a naturally demonstrative person. So when she patted Tula's hand, the moment meant something. "But why all the secrecy? You have to know your family will be over the moon excited for you."

"Until I tell them I want to write fulltime." Since Tula's confession didn't cause the walls to crash around her, she pressed her luck. "*Full*time."

"Oh." The light dawned in Zoe's eyes. "You don't want to teach."

"I don't want to teach."

Until Tula spoke the truth to her family, she knew the weight on her chest wouldn't ease completely. However, once she took Zoe into her confidence, she felt lighter than she had in months.

"Smith..." Tula shrugged. For some reason, fair or not, she always focused her worries on her brother.

"Is awfully proud of his little sister," Zoe finished for her. "The first time he brought me here to meet the Carson clan, Smith said those very words. I imagine you've heard them, and several variations, more times than you can count."

"You understand." Tula forced the short sentence past the emotional lump in her throat.

"I think so." Zoe nodded. Then took Tula by the arm. "You might want to sit before you fall down."

Until Zoe alerted her to the fact, Tula hadn't realized her locked knees were the only things between her and a face plant onto the bedroom floor. Legs a bit wobbly, she flopped onto the mattress.

"When I started college, I was completely focused on teaching. Excited. Committed."

"Passionate?" Zoe asked.

"Maybe."

Focused for so long, Tula couldn't remember how she'd felt as a fresh-faced eighteen-year-old. She'd had goals. And met every one. Complete her bachelor's degree in three years. Check. Master's degree in less than two years. Check. And then? Panic had set in.

"Do you know why I decided to get my Ph.D.?"

"So Smith would have to call you Dr. Tula?"

Tula smiled at Zoe's joke.

"A nice bonus, but no. I was afraid. Scared witless." Tula's palms dampened at the memory. "I was only twenty-three. I hadn't done anything outside of a classroom. I hadn't lived. And what did I see in my future?"

"More classrooms?"

"Yes!" Tula groaned. "Then and there, I should have come clean with my family. Shared my doubts. My fears. Instead, I shoved my head in the sand and my butt back in class for three more years."

Zoe chuckled. And Tula joined her.

"Crazy, huh?"

"I don't know," Zoe shrugged. "You've accomplished a lot, Tula. Maybe one day you'll decide to teach. Maybe not. But one thing is for certain."

"What?"

"You wrote a hit song."

A grin burst onto Tula's face.

"I wrote a hit song."

"How did *Crazy Day* end up in Fleet Sherman's hands?"

Like a burst dam, the story poured from Tula in a steady flow of words and emotions. She told Zoe about the songs she wrote in secret—for years. About the contest. How Fleet showed up at her door. Plus, everything in between. And after.

"Fleet took a chance on me," Tula said when she finally wound down.

"Fleet Sherman gave you a hand up," Zoe corrected. "Exactly what your brother would have done if you'd let him."

"Like Ryder did for you?"

Tula felt ashamed the second the words left her mouth. Nobody in the music industry could accuse Zoe Hart of riding her brother's coattails to the top.

Zoe didn't seem the least bit concerned.

"I'm the only woman in a rock band named after my brother. Naturally, I heard claims of nepotism. I kept my mouth shut." Zoe smiled, a glint in her eyes. "And let my talent do the talking."

"I wish I had your confidence," Tula sighed. "About everything."

A frown creased her brow as she turned her head toward Tula.

"Have we switched topics?"

"Yes and no."

Tula had spilled her guts on the subject of her secret songwriting. Anything else should have been a breeze. Yet, she hesitated.

"Don't stop now," Zoe urged. "You're on a spill your guts roll."

"How well do you know Fleet Sherman?"

"Not well. We cross paths now and then."

"Did he ever…" Tula struggled to find the right words. "Hit on you?"

"Not that I can remember." Zoe sat up like a bolt, a sharp look of concern in her dark eyes. "Why? What did he do?"

"Nothing." Tula rushed to Fleet's defense. "He's been a perfect gentleman."

Zoe relaxed. "The music world is surprisingly small. And people talk. I've never heard anything bad about how Fleet treats women."

"Fleet is kind. And considerate. In a short time, he's taught me so much." Tula reached down for her last reserve of courage. "And sometimes I want to rip his clothes off and have my way with him. Which would be difficult since most of the time, he's in a different city."

"Phone sex is safer than a condom."

"My confession doesn't surprise you?"

"Surprised proximity to Fleet Sherman has you hot and bothered? Hardly. The man is sex on a stick. He's also notoriously commitment shy."

"I don't want to get married. I want..." Tula fanned herself. "I *want*. Unfortunately, Fleet doesn't feel the same."

"Right." Zoe seemed to find the idea hilarious. When Tula didn't join in, she sobered. "You're serious?"

"Look at me."

Tula spun around. Zoe looked her up, down, and sideways. And frowned.

"What?"

For a second, Tula had forgotten Zoe wouldn't understand. Her gorgeous future sister-in-law didn't walk amongst the mere mortals of the world.

"*You* inspire lust. *I* inspire a handshake."

Tula didn't want sympathy. Facts were facts. She'd come to terms with her lack of sex appeal long ago. Or thought she had. Until Fleet.

"How do I generate a little *va-va-voom*?

"You have plenty of *va* in your *voom*, Tula. However." Zoe held up a hand before Tula could protest. "I don't expect you to take my word. And despite what you think, I'm not in tune with the sexual side of the male psyche."

Tula didn't buy it.

"You and Smith can't keep your hands off each other."

"Smith isn't every man. He's mine." Zoe let out a happy sigh. "And we click. However, if you want my advice?"

"Please."

"You have to make the first move."

"Physically or verbally?" Tula couldn't imagine either.

"Tell Fleet what you want, Tula." Zoe stood and stretched. "If he's interested, he'll take care of the rest. And don't doubt he'll be very interested."

"Or, he might laugh his ass off."

"You're strong. Independent. If Fleet doesn't want you, you'll survive. If he laughs. Let me know." Zoe lifted her foot to show off gray leather and a spiked heel. "These boots aren't just made for walking."

"I appreciate the offer. However, if Fleet needs a good ball kicking, I can handle the task by myself."

"I have no doubt."

"Thanks." Tula hugged Zoe and sighed. "I guess now's the time to talk to my family."

"You want to start with Smith." A statement, not a question. And right on target. Tula nodded just as her phone rang.

"Fleet?" Zoe asked.

"How'd you know?"

"The look on your face. Nerves and excitement." Zoe smiled, closing the door behind her.

Tula took a deep breath. She hit accept, took one look at Fleet's handsome face, and for the first time since they'd met, she was at a loss. Attraction or no attraction, she could talk to him for hours on end. And he could talk to her. Back and forth. Never a lull.

Until now, when Tula needed her words more than ever. Luckily, Fleet had no idea what was—or wasn't—on her mind.

"We're number one," Fleet blurted out.

Tula blinked. Her heart tried to leap from her chest. And she completely forgot why she was supposed to have a massive case of nerves.

"No," she gasped. "How can you be sure? I didn't think the new *Billboard* charts came out until Tuesday."

"If you know the right people, and I do, you can get the news early. Congratulations, you're a—"

"I'm going to throw up."

"Not the reaction I hoped for." Fleet chuckled. "Find a toilet. Quick."

Tula rushed from the bedroom. As she ran down the hall, praying with every step the bathroom wasn't occupied, she passed a startled Zoe. With no preamble, she shoved the phone into the startled blonde's hand and slammed the door behind her.

CHAPTER SIX

"HELLO?" RIDICULOUSLY, FLEET tried to peer around the corner as if he could see beyond the confines of his iPad screen. "Tula? Are you okay?"

"Tula is indisposed."

"Well, Zoe Hart." Fleet didn't know what to think when he saw the dark-eyed beauty's face looking back at him. "What an unexpected and happy surprise."

"Fleet." Zoe didn't return his smile.

Unsure what to say, Fleet tried to think of a reason he would call Tula when her family had no idea they wrote together, let alone had ever met. He hadn't meant to stick Tula in an uncomfortable situation. Then again, he couldn't have anticipated her reaction to his news.

"Happy Thanksgiving."

Silently, Fleet groaned. Of all the lame excuses, he may have hit on the lamest. The twist of Zoe's lips and the look of disbelief in her eyes told him he was right.

"You can relax," Zoe shook her head with a sigh. "Tula told me everything."

"What's everything?" Fleet knew how to keep a secret. And he was familiar with all the tactics used to flush out information. Until Zoe shared some concrete details, he wouldn't spill a single bean.

"Don't be cute, Fleet. I know all about you and Tula."

"What about my sister and Fleet Sherman?"

Smith Carson loomed over Zoe's shoulder, his puzzled expression grim. *Very, very* grim. *Well, shit*, Fleet thought. He rubbed a hand over the stubble on his unshaven cheeks. He was a man who avoided uncomfortable situations like the plague. He had enough family conflict in his childhood to last a lifetime.

However, when trouble was at hand, Fleet didn't run. Especially when someone he cared about needed his protection.

"Lay a finger on Tula, and I will turn your pretty face to a pulp."

"What the fuck?" Smith grabbed the phone, his face inches from the screen, his blue eyes stormy. "Where do you get off, asshole? I would never hurt Tula or any woman. Why would you suggest such a thing?"

Sometimes distance was a good thing. If Fleet had Smith Carson in the same room, he would happily wrap his hands around the bastard's throat.

"Tula hasn't told you about me. She must have a good reason. Fear comes to mind."

"Tula isn't afraid of me," Smith ground out. "And what about you? Zoe? What the hell is going on?"

"I'll tell you, Smith."

"Tula?" Fleet called out when he heard her voice. "Are you okay? Damn it! Let me see you."

"Everything is fine, Fleet. My brother is a jerk. Not for the first time in his life. Smith. Be a good boy and give me my phone."

Tula didn't sound afraid of her brother. In fact, the only emotion Fleet could detect in her voice was a large dose of sisterly exasperation.

Fleet's limited view of the situation suddenly shifted from Smith Carson's angry expression to the floor and a pair of black, well-worn, lace-up work boots.

"You can have the phone." The edge to Smith's voice was sharp. "*After* you explain what the hell is going on between you and Fleet Sherman."

"If you don't change your tone, I won't tell you a freaking thing," Tula shot back. "Smith. If you hang up, I swear I'll—"

"Tula?" Fleet called her name just as the screen went black.

Son of a bitch. Fleet hurled the pad across the room. A definitive cracking sound followed a thud as the device hit the wall, leaving a sizable dent. He didn't give a shit about collateral damage. All he could think about was Tula.

Fleet began to pace the confines of his home office. Back and forth as his brain tried to calculate the time and distance he would need to travel to get to Tula.

She's okay, Fleet assured himself. Hands clammy, he wiped them on the front of his jeans. Though he hadn't experienced the feeling in seven years. Not since the court system finally locked his father away in a much-deserved cage. He recognized the queasy unease in the pit of his stomach.

Fear. Frustration. Helplessness. When Fleet was a young boy, he'd been too small, too weak to stop his father's abuse. The last time, after he'd convinced his mother to leave the bastard and foolishly believed she was safe, he'd been too far away to prevent the bone-crushing beating which landed her in the hospital.

The police assured Fleet even if he'd been in the same town instead of on tour, he couldn't have stopped what happened. The assurances hadn't helped. Right or wrong, Fleet had lived with the guilt ever since.

Logic told him Tula would be fine. Their childhoods had been worlds apart. *Her* father honored and loved his wife. His children. Her brother raised his voice, not his fist. She wasn't in pain. She didn't need him to rush to her defense.

However, a big disconnect existed between Fleet's brain and logic. Understandable, he supposed.

His iPad out of commission, Fleet quickly checked his phone. He let out a sigh of relief when the screen jumped to life. Full service. One hundred percent charged.

"Then why the hell hasn't Tula called me back?"

Fleet decided to give Tula ten minutes. If he hadn't heard from her, he might give her another ten. Small increments were doable, he decided. If he started to think about the hours, he would drive himself crazy.

To save his sanity, Fleet picked up his guitar, sat at his desk, strummed the first few chords of a new melody, and kept his back to the clock.

Eyes closed, Fleet let his fingers take over. The action familiar. Soothing. As note followed note, he hummed along. Muscles—neck, shoulders, back—loosened. Unconsciously, as Fleet played, he entered new musical territory. Until Tula's song, the material he wrote and recorded sported a hard, some might say cynical, viewpoint. Even love songs—rare in his catalog of hits—were edgier than most in the genre.

Fleet Sherman didn't do romance. Personally or professionally. However, as the body of the song took shape, he had no control over the direction. The rhythm, the mood, was designed to draw the listener in. Slowly, but inexorably. Sexy, but not overtly so. A subtle sensuality.

Exactly like Tula.

The thought was so out of the blue, Fleet froze. The implications so far-reaching, he dropped his guitar as if the strings had turned to fire. *What the hell?* Tula was his friend. His writing partner. He wanted to work with her, not sleep with her.

True, Fleet went a little crazy when he thought Tula was in danger. Maybe his stomach hadn't settled completely. And so what if he looked at the phone—willing her unique ringtone to sound—a dozen or so times. Fleet wanted to protect her. As he would any woman. Any *person* in a similar situation. Not with as much passion, he admitted. Or as much...

Well, shit. With a sigh, he rested his head against the high-backed chair. When necessary, Fleet would fudge the truth. But he never lied to himself. He wanted Tula Carson. Beautiful, smart, unquestionably talented, Tula.

Tula had come out of nowhere. Blindsided him. For the life of him, Fleet didn't know what to think.

"Yes, you do." Remember, son. Honesty is the best policy. "You know what you want. And you know what you can't have."

Fleet *wanted* to have sex with Tula. Often and in a variety of creative ways. He figured a week in bed with her body wrapped around his should get the need out of his system. Probably. The problem? Because they worked together, and on a certain level, she worked *for* him, Fleet couldn't—*wouldn't* touch—Tula unless she made the first move.

"Tula isn't the type to jump my bones." Fleet scrubbed a hand over his face. "And, *I* am royally screwed."

Fleet figured he should savor the feeling. Where Tula was concerned, *royally screwed* was as close as he would get to the real thing.

Not sure whether to laugh or thumb through his list of willing and available bed partners, Fleet didn't have time to decide as the opening bars of *Brown Eyed Girl* filled the office.

"Tula?" Fleet scanned her face for visible signs of trauma.

"Fleet." Tula sounded as relieved as he felt. "I was afraid you'd given up on me. After Smith's meltdown, I wouldn't have blamed you."

"Did he hurt you?"

"Who? Smith?" Tula laughed. "Are you serious?"

"Yes."

"Oh." Consternation entered her dark gaze. "I forgot about your mother. I'm sorry, Fleet."

Fleet never, never shared the details of his childhood. Tula turned out to be the exception. He hadn't meant to tell her. They'd fallen into the habit of sharing bits and pieces from their pasts. Tula was such a good listener, the words flowed with a natural ease he never could have anticipated. And once he started, he couldn't hold back.

"Tell me you're okay, Tula."

She looked good. Great. Perfect. But Fleet needed the words.

"My brother has the growl of a grizzly, but the claws of a teddy bear. I promise I'm fine, Fleet.

The warmth in Tula's smile reached through the phone and covered him like the softest blanket imaginable. Convinced, Fleet's worry shifted from her physical safety to his over-active libido. Down boy, he cautioned his dick.

"Your family cares about you? They would never hurt you?"

"Never."

"Then why all the secrecy? Why not tell them you wrote the fucking song?"

A myriad of emotions passed across Tula's face. She landed on confusion.

"Are you angry?"

"I guess I am." And horny. And frustrated. And Fleet had no problem dumping the blame on Tula. "You told me a lot about yourself, Tula. But you remained reticent about one thing."

"The song."

"The song," Fleet agreed. "And the contest. If the subject related to music and your family, you clammed up. Why?"

"Fear." Tula shook her head. "I wouldn't expect you to understand."

"Try me."

"I didn't want to disappoint them. My parents. My siblings. Smith, especially. I was destined to teach, and they were so proud. I dreaded the look in their eyes when they found out the truth."

Fleet was hit by a flash of empathy. Which surprised the hell out of him. He didn't know a thing about big family dynamics. But he knew one thing.

"You can't live your life by other people's expectations, Tula."

"I tried. And ultimately, failed. So, I only had one course of action."

Tula met Fleet's gaze. Steady. Sure.

"The truth?"

"The truth." Tula's chuckle was laced with wonder. "I just spilled my guts to my family. From start to finish. I told them everything. And do you know what?"

Her story to tell, Fleet decided. However, from the expression on Tula's face, he could figure out the ending.

"Mom cried. She was proud of our number one song. And thrilled I have a degree to fall back on."

"Sounds like a typical mother."

"Dad reminded everyone *he'd* passed along the music gene. And Smith?" Tula looked a little teary herself. "He was still angry. Because I didn't give him first crack at *Crazy Day*."

Fleet could relate. A good song was more precious than diamonds. And twice as hard to find.

"Okay."

"Okay? Really?" Tula's eyes narrowed. "You don't have anything else to say?"

Prudently, Fleet held his tongue. What he wanted to say would send Tula running into the Alabama hills.

"Fleet?"

"Hmm?"

"Say something."

"When can we fit in a writing session?" Safe, solid, neutral ground. "If we can agree on the final bridge, I'll debut *Take it Back* in Los Angeles on December tenth."

"Well..." Tula's gaze darted from side to side as if she didn't have the nerve to look him in the eyes.

"Damn it, Tula. Did you let your brother talk you out of writing with me?" A wave of emotion—part panic, part anger, part something he didn't want to identify—zipped through Fleet. Since he understood anger, he took the less treacherous road. "You take a big step toward thinking for yourself, then backtrack as soon as idiot boy applies a little pressure."

"Smith suggested he and I should try our hands at a song together. However, Mr. Carson," her tone quickly changed from giddy to annoyed. "I always think for myself. And Smith isn't the only idiot. Do us all a favor and look in the mirror."

Tula's cheeks flushed a pretty pink, her lips parted slightly, her breathing heavy. Fleet groaned as he covertly checked his chin for drool.

"I *always* want to write with you," Tula snapped. "Today. Tomorrow. Until the words run dry."

"Good to know." Great. Fantastic. Best news ever. "Why did you hesitate?"

"Skyping is nice, but I miss the connection we get when we're in the same room. My schedule is free. You name the time and place."

"My place. Monday." Fleet spoke before he could think. Yup. He was definitely an idiot. "Unless you'd rather not. Vermont isn't exactly around the corner."

"You don't mind if I invade your inner sanctum?"

Inner sanctum? Fleet snorted. He freaking loved the way Tula's superior mind worked.

"Consider yourself welcome anytime, Tula." Fleet would have to put his raging hormones on ice. "I'll send my plane for you."

"You will not." Tula sounded as appalled as she looked. "I can get to Vermont on my own dime, thank you very much."

"I could argue."

"And waste both our time? No."

Fleet had butted heads enough times with his mother to recognize intractable. Fiona Sherman spent years as a man's powerless punching bag. No more. Once she found her voice, she refused to stay silent. Fleet wished she would let him win an argument now and then. However, he knew better than anyone what she'd suffered and was happy to cheer her on.

"At least let me pay for your ticket."

"My dime, Fleet." Tula rolled her eyes. "Jeez. And don't offer to send a car. I'll hitchhike."

"Not funny, Petula Joyce." Joke or no joke, Fleet shuddered at the thought. "Am I at least allowed to text you the address?"

Tula's lips twitched.

"Please. I'll see you Monday."

Fleet set his phone on the desk. He had three days to figure out how he would sit next to Tula without developing an inconvenient erection.

Get your shit together, Sherman. You aren't a kid even though Tula suddenly made him feel sixteen and untried.

Fleet stared at the ceiling and sighed. *I wonder if saltpeter really works.*

CHAPTER SEVEN

TULA WAS LATE. Her flight had been like clockwork. They landed early—for once. She and her carry-on bag had found the car rental agency with little fuss or muss.

Then Tula made two mistakes. She left the airport. And she relied on the annoying robot-voiced navigation system instead of a good old-fashioned map. To say the drive to Fleet's house hadn't been as smooth as the first leg of her trip would be putting it mildly.

After Tula drove down the wrong street for the third time, she did what any intelligent, rational woman would do. She stopped for directions.

"Excuse me." Slightly frazzled, Tula tried to muster a winning smile for the man behind the convenience store counter. "I think I missed my turnoff. Can you tell me how to get to 1267 Sterling Lane?

The stubble on his face stark white, if the man's stooped shoulders and frail body were any indications, he must have seen at least ninety summers. However, he could still muster a twinkle in his faded blue eyes.

"Most of Fleet's fans just want me to point them in the right direction. You managed to come up with an address." The noise the man made was more of a cackle than a laugh. "Not that you have the right one, mind you. But you get points for originality."

Ready to laugh—at anything, including herself—Tula felt her good humor return. Honestly, she hadn't considered how her request would sound. Fleet Sherman fell into the rarified mega-famous category. He'd lived just outside of Millersburg for over six years. By now, the townspeople were undoubtedly old hats at dealing with his adoring fans.

Tula upped the wattage on her smile. She had to give the man credit. He could make a pretty penny if he wanted to sell the local celebrity's address. Instead, he guarded Fleet's location. Admirable indeed.

"Do you know Fleet, Mr....?"

"Name's Argyle. No mister attached. As for Fleet. Maybe I know him. And maybe I don't." Cagey, the old man looked Tula up and down. "You have an intelligent face. Why do you want to spend your time chasing a pretty face? Or are you one of those *reporters*?"

Argyle spit the word out like the foulest curse. *Yikes*, Tula thought. Whether through prejudice or experience, she imagined he had a tale or two to tell. However, she didn't have time to listen.

"Thank you for your time, Argyle. I'll be sure and tell Fleet how diligent you are with his privacy."

"Wait," Argyle called out as Tula left the store. "Do *you* know Fleet?"

Tula turned and winked.

"Maybe I do, and maybe I don't."

And maybe—if I don't lose my nerve—by tonight, I'll know him a whole lot better.

"YOU SHOULD HAVE called me."

"I did. Eventually. I would have been fine if the GPS in my rental car had recognized your address."

"You're here now." Fleet smiled. "Welcome."

Tula watched as Fleet removed her suitcase from the trunk. His hair was messy and slightly damp—she must have caught him in the middle of a workout. *My, oh, my.* Tula mentally fanned herself. Sweaty Fleet was just sexy as fresh as a daisy Fleet.

He wore a pair of low-riding, dark-blue sweats, and a long-sleeved t-shirt which proclaimed his love for fast cars and bourbon.

The cars, Tula understood. He'd mentioned he had a nice collection of what he called his foreign beauties. But the booze?

She'd never seen Fleet take a drink. He turned down the beer she offered.

She supposed his reticence had to do with his father, but she couldn't be sure. As open as Fleet was about his tumultuous childhood, he didn't elaborate about Mick Sherman. He didn't call him Dad. Or Mick. *That bastard* was the term Fleet preferred. And from what he'd shared with Tula, she didn't blame him a bit.

"Argyle phoned a few minutes after I heard from you." Fleet sent Tula a roguish grin. "He told me, and I quote, 'Watch out for the dark-eyed beauty, boy. Seemed nice enough, mind you. But *that* one looks like she means business. Mark my words. Before you know what happened, her sweet smile will get you into a heap of trouble.' End quote."

"Trouble? Me?"

Tula was inordinately pleased by Argyle's description. Dark-eyed beauty was flattering. But nobody thought of her as a disruptive force. Until now. She planned to tuck the compliment away like a treasured keepsake.

"Argyle is a worrier. I assured him we were friends. After I told him he'd hit the nail on the head." As Fleet curled a strand of her long hair around his finger—something he'd never done before—a crease formed between his brows. "Trouble with a capital T."

Fleet's last words were said in a thick, muttered, Irish brogue. Tula held her breath, certain he would kiss her. The moment felt right. Charged with tension of the sexual variety. Or so she hoped. However, before she could lean closer, Fleet dropped her hair as if the ends suddenly burned his fingers.

"Come on." Fleet backed away and motioned for Tula to precede him. "Let's get out of the cold and into the warm house. I'll move your car into the garage after lunch."

Disappointed the moment had gotten away from her, Tula nodded. She had to admit, the weather was a bit nippy compared to Alabama. Though her parents' farm was high enough in the hills to get a fair covering of snow—just in time for some holiday magic—November in Vermont was an entirely different animal.

Tula put her hands in the pockets of her sturdy winter coat and walked down the cobbled path. The grounds were huge. From the gated entrance to the surrounding trees, color burst from every corner. Fall leaves from the palest yellow to the deepest red fell to the ground in a typical haphazard pattern.

Hearty perennials which Tula recognized from her mother's garden filled every well-tended bed. Wild yet contained was the best way to describe what she saw. Fleet hadn't conquered the wilderness. He chose to co-exist with nature. And Tula heartily approved.

Tula ran her hand over the solid doorjamb.

"Was the house here when you bought the property?"

"*A* house." Fleet closed the front door. He put Tula's suitcase near the winding staircase. "More of a decaying shack. I was happy to start from the ground up."

Fleet hadn't used his chance to start from scratch to build a modern monstrosity. Large in scale, but a simpler, more laidback aesthetic.

Colonial in design, until she took a closer look, Tula would have guessed the house stood for centuries. She recognized hand-hewn boards when she saw them. When the time had come to replace the original flooring in the Carson home, her father—with the help of her brothers—had cut, shaped, sanded, and installed every piece of wood.

"Do you ever get lost?" Tula teased. She hung her coat on a wrought-iron rack and followed Fleet from the living room to the kitchen. "Your house is huge."

As was the kitchen. Unlike many modern designs, the room wasn't open to the rest of the house. Large. Airy. But private. The same as where her mother cooked meals for her family. Much more luxurious. But just as warm and welcoming, Tula thought with appreciation.

The appliances looked like something out of as 1940s movie—updated, naturally. Cabinets and countertops gleamed. As did the travertine floor and subway tile backsplash. For the first time in her life, Tula experienced a major case of kitchen envy.

"I grew up in a one-bedroom flat on the second floor of a Dublin tenement. Tight quarters would be a generous description. The walls were thin. My old man's temper thinner." Fleet wasn't out for sympathy. His shrug was matter of fact. "I felt trapped."

Tula grew up with nothing but space. Though the house was filled to near bursting, she could go outside anytime she wanted, walk for miles, clear her head, and return to a place where she felt safe.

"May I ask you a question?"

"Any secret I might have left isn't worth knowing." Fleet chuckled. "Shoot."

"How did you turn out so…?" Tula searched for a delicate turn of phrase. "Undamaged?"

"Undamaged. Good word. However, I wouldn't say your assessment is entirely accurate." Without asking, Fleet set two cups on the counter. "I was screwed up, Tula. In some ways, maybe I still am. I've worked hard to be a better man than the bastard who sired me. Most days, I like to think I succeed."

Without warning, Tula's eyes filled. Distressed, she tried to turn away. She didn't think Fleet would appreciate her tears even though she cried for the emotionally scarred boy, not the strong, confident man.

"Here now." Fleet was around the butcher-block island before Tula could wipe away the first tear. Gently, he smoothed the wetness from her cheek, his head bent until his hazel eyes were level with hers. "Do I strike you as a man in need of sympathy?"

Inches away, Tula could feel the heat from Fleet's body. His heady scent—clean sweat and something mouthwateringly spicy—made her blood race through her veins like wildfire.

"You don't need anybody's sympathy." Tula bucked up her courage. "However, I hope you need this."

Tula started with a tentative brush of her lips across Fleet's. As much as she wanted him, she refused to throw herself at him—literally or otherwise. If they were together, the decision had to be mutual.

Fleet took a deep, ragged breath. He didn't touch her. Nor did he pull away. A good sign in Tula's estimation. The flecks in his eyes weren't green. Or gold. Whatever the color, they were as bright as a cloudless, star-filled night sky.

"Not a good idea, darlin'."

Tula's heart sank.

"Because you don't want me?"

"Because I want you *too* much." With a sigh, Fleet rested his forehead against hers. "I'm a bad bet, Tula. Sex, I can do. Happily. Enthusiastically. With a bit of skill, so I'm told."

"Sounds good to me." Better than good. If Tula had her way, they would already be naked and halfway to the bedroom.

"I promised myself I wouldn't take advantage."

"What advantage?" Tula was confused.

"I'm older."

"By three years."

When Fleet moved away, Tula wanted to cry out with frustration. She wanted to reach out. Hold on for all she was worth. Hadn't she done as Zoe advised? Bucked up her courage. Made the first move. Fleet was supposed to fall into her plan. Instead, he wanted to find excuses why they shouldn't be together.

Hardly a boost to Tula's rapidly fraying ego.

"I have more experience." His tone reasonable, Fleet turned on the electric kettle.

"I'll give you that one." Tula sighed. "I'm not a virgin, Fleet. I've been with a man."

Fleet's lips quirked. Apparently, the idea amused him.

"Only one?" he chuckled.

"Yes."

No reason to lie, Tula mused. One lover or a hundred, she was who she was. Bold. Unapologetic. She met Fleet's gaze. And witnessed the second her words sank in.

"Oh." Fleet sobered. "Well, shit, Tula."

Minutes earlier, passion put the heat in her blood. Now? Anger. And to her surprise, she liked the feeling.

"Suddenly I'm not good enough for you?" Eyes blazing, Tula tossed her hands in the air. "What's the cutoff point for the great Fleet Sherman? How much experience is enough to qualify me for entrance into your bed?"

"Don't be ridiculous."

"I'm serious. One is obviously too few. Is ten enough? Twenty?"

"Stop, Tula."

Fleet sounded as angry as Tula felt. *Good*, she thought. At least they'd found *one* emotion they could share.

"We have a number," Tula exclaimed. "Twenty men and I can join the, *I slept with Fleet Sherman* club. Hardly exclusive. But what the hell. I'm game. *After* I find nineteen random men to fill my quota."

Jaw clenched, Fleet gripped the counter until his knuckles turned white. He closed his eyes and breathed. In. Out. In. Out. Deep, calming breaths. Fascinated, Tula found herself doing the same. The anger drained from Fleet's body. And from hers.

When Fleet raised his lids, his gaze was cool.

"Are you finished?"

"I don't know. Am I?"

Tula didn't wait for an answer. She'd taken herself on an emotional rollercoaster. Highs and lows. Dips and curves. Fleet had been along for the ride. Her unwilling passenger.

The blame was firmly on Tula's shoulders, not Fleet's. She covered her face with her hands.

"I feel like a fool."

"Tula..."

"Don't be nice to me, Fleet." Tula felt so low she couldn't even muster up a good old-fashioned, cleansing cry. "I swear I'll break into a million pieces."

"Please don't. My cleaning lady would kill me."

"A joke? Really?" In spite of herself, Tula smiled. Tentative. A bit shaky. But a genuine smile. *Unbelievable.* "You really *are* charming. Why can't you be a mouth-breathing Neanderthal? And smell bad?"

As Tula peered through her fingers, Fleet flashed his irresistible smile.

"Anything else?" he asked.

Sure, Tula thought. She could go on and on. *If* she wanted to embarrass herself even further. *And* feel his ego.

"I'll send you a list."

"Not necessary." Fleet rubbed the back of his neck, his brow furrowed in thought. His eyes—damn those eyes—stared at her for what seemed like forever. "If we're going to do this, you need to say the words."

"The words?" Tula wondered if she'd missed a part of the conversation.

Fleet peeled Tula's hands from her face. "The words, Tula."

"You want me to sink a level lower and beg? Nope. Sorry, pal. Not going to happen."

Tula tried to jerk her hands from his. Fleet simply shook his head. Too emotionally drained to argue, she let him have his way. *This time.* Instead of a useless tussle, she sent him a dirty look.

"I thought you were kind," Tula huffed.

"You were mistaken." Eyes locked with hers, Fleet raised her hand to his lips. "I want you, Tula. More than you can know. But I won't make another move until you say the words."

"I already did." *Didn't she?*

Slowly, Fleet shook his head. Tula tried to remember.

"I know I kissed you. A major milestone for me, by the way. And..." The scene flashed through Tula's mind. "You didn't kiss me back."

"But what did I say?"

"*Not a good idea, darlin'.*" Tula's brogue wasn't perfect, but under the circumstances, close enough.

"You remember the wrong part, Tula." Fleet's gold-flecked eyes heated. "I said I want you."

Tula's heartbeat stuttered. Before she raced ahead, she had to make certain they were headed down the same road.

"You said you wanted me too much. What does too much mean?"

"I don't want to hurt you. I sure as hell know I'm not good enough for you. I don't take what isn't freely offered. But make no mistake, I'm no saint. If you want me? *Say. The. Words.*"

The Irish in Fleet's voice whispered across Tula's skin like a warm summer's breeze. He left the rest up to her. If she wanted the heated promise in his eyes, she had to be the one to jump.

Tula had come so far. She'd be a fool to turn back now. She didn't hesitate. She said the words.

"I want you, Fleet Sherman." Confident and a bit cocky, Tula tipped her head to one side. "Now, what are you going to do about it?"

Fleet didn't give Tula time to bask in her womanly allure. He took her in his arms and kissed her. Not a tentative, fumbling, exploratory little peck. A full-on, I know exactly what I'm doing, buckle your seatbelt, holy crap, kiss.

For a second, Tula panicked. She was out of her depth. A second later, she didn't care. Fleet had everything under control. However, he soon let her know he expected more than a passive participant. He wouldn't settle for anything less than a kiss for a kiss. A touch for a touch.

Tula gasped. She'd never been bitten. On the neck. Or anyplace. Not during sex. She didn't know if she approved. Then, Fleet bit her again. *Holy crap*. She definitely approved. Everything felt so new. So wonderful. So intimidating.

"I don't want to disappoint you."

"Don't worry. Be yourself. Be with me. Here. Now. In the moment." An arm around her waist, Fleet nuzzled her ear. "I can't get enough of you."

Magic. In Fleet's voice. In his kiss. In him. He made her want things she'd only read about. Things she never would have considered with another man. Her sexual horizons had always seemed barren. Boring. With Fleet? The sky wasn't the limit. Only the beginning.

"I need to see you. All of you."

The intensity of Fleet's gaze made Tula a little nervous. In a good way. His touch left a trail of tingling skin. She felt open to all possibilities.

No more boring little Tula. The wild woman in her was ready to break free. Finally.

Tula's shirt sailed over Fleet's shoulder. Smiling, he traced the strap of her lacy pink bra.

"Very nice."

Tula refused to blush, though she couldn't stop a trace of color from staining her cheeks.

Fleet might not remember the day they met and her less than alluring bra. Tula did. Maybe new underwear had boosted her confidence. Maybe not. Either way, she was here. With Fleet. Halfway to naked. A little sexy never hurt.

"Lace or plain white cotton. You're gorgeous, Tula."

He remembered. Tula's heart constricted in an unfamiliar way. More of a stutter than a skipped beat. Interesting. However, she didn't have time to think about the implications. Fleet slipped to his knees. She'd never had a man literally at her feet. Let alone one with an angel's smile and the devil in his eyes. She wanted to savor every moment.

Fleet kissed Tula's bare stomach. With a moan, her head fell back. Her fingers threaded through his thick, dark hair. She would worry about her heart later. Fleet kissed her again. *Much* later.

Her boots hit the floor. Her socks soon followed. Fleet tugged her pants over her hips.

"Whoever invented leggings was a genius. Easy access." Slowly, almost reverently, he pushed the material down Tula's legs. "Must have been a man."

"Or a woman who imagined the person in her life exactly as you are now."

The familiar twinkle in his hazel gaze, Fleet looked up, before his focus returned to his task at hand.

"Is everything about sex?"

"No… Ohhhhh." Tula's eyes sprang open. Whatever Fleet was up to, she approved wholeheartedly.

"Say again?" Fleet teased—with his words and his fingers. "No? Yes?"

The best Tula could gasp was a faint, *I don't know.*

"Poor Tula. Cat got your tongue?"

Tula nodded, and Fleet grinned.

"Then I'll answer for you. Everything isn't about sex." He punctuated each word with a strategically placed kiss. "However, if done properly? The proper kiss? The proper touch? The proper penetration? Sex falls damn close to the top of *my* list."

Fleet's hand disappeared beneath the pink lace material. And Tula's legs gave out. Without missing a beat, he caught her before her knees slammed onto the tile floor.

For balance, and because she wanted to touch him, Tula wrapped her arms around Fleet's neck. He took a moment to kiss her. Long. Slow. As far from sweet as Tula had ever ventured. When Fleet lifted his head, she ran her tongue over her bottom lip. Slowly. She didn't want to waste a bit of his intoxicating taste.

"Well?" Fleet's mouth brushed against Tula's ear.

Tula shivered. "Very well. Thank you."

Fleet chuckled. "Good to hear. But I wanted your opinion on my kiss. My touch. My…" His fingers moved deeper. "Penetration. Properly done? Yes? Or no?"

Yes. Yes. And yes again. Tula shouted the words in her head. For Fleet's benefit, she merely shrugged.

"I need more time to decide."

Eyebrow raised, Fleet looked interested.

"How much time?"

"A minute? No. An hour." Tula bit her lip when Fleet's free hand caressed the sensitive skin of her inner thigh. *Holy crap.* "Can you get back to me at the end of the day?"

"We'll leave the question open ended. Today. Tomorrow. Next week."

Tula expected to break into a million pieces any second. An entire week of Fleet and his magic touch might be the end of her. Though she couldn't think of a better way to go.

And then the world turned upside down. And on its side. A whirlwind roared through Tula's body. A cacophony of colors swam before her eyes. She knew how an orgasm felt. *This*? The explosion of pure pleasure? Somebody had to invent a new word. She had entered a new realm of bliss.

CHAPTER EIGHT

FOR A MOMENT, Tula wondered if the earth had actually moved. Her body felt as light as her head. Then the pleasure fog lifted long enough to realize she was in Fleet's arms, not floating on a cloud.

Through the kitchen and up the long staircase, he carried her with impressive ease. Had she fainted? *Embarrassing*. But she didn't care. She'd trade a little mortification for the kind of wild pleasure she hadn't—until now—believed existed outside the pages of a book.

Fleet seemed happy with the turn of events. Smug would be the best way to describe his expression.

"You look pleased with yourself."

"And why not?" The Irish in Fleet's voice almost hid the smug. But not quite. "I've never blissed a woman into unconsciousness before. And without my big gun in the game."

Tula snorted. Funny man. Then, as he gently tossed her onto the bed, a worrisome thought popped into her head. Fleet's sweatpants were loose, but they couldn't conceal the sizable bulge between his legs. She was more than interested. Still…

"Exactly how big a gun are we talking about?"

"I can give you a preview if you like." Fleet toyed with the waistband of his sweats. "However, I can guarantee I don't have more than you can take."

"How do you know?" Tula asked. Wide eyed—if not exactly innocent—she batted her lashes. She wasn't worried about size. Or fit. Not really. But she enjoyed their teasing banter too much to stop now.

"I made an exploratory journey." Fleet wiggled his magic fingers. And grinned. "I can state with great confidence, we'll both enjoy my... how shall I say? My *foray* into your practically uncharted territory."

Lordy, Lordy, he was cute. Sexy as all get out. Mouthwatering from head to toe. Tula wondered if Fleet knew his appeal went far beyond the physical. He made her laugh. And happy. She trusted him to treat her right—in and out of bed. With enough money and time, almost anybody could acquire a pretty face and a toned body. Fleet's best attributes couldn't be bought. He—and they—were priceless.

Fleet toed off his shoes. He reached for the hem of his shirt.

Still dressed in her bra and undies, Tula propped herself up on her elbows and nodded. If he wanted to put on a show, who was she to argue? Only one thing was missing.

"Where's the music?"

81

"Your wish is my command."

Tula expected a short break while Fleet cued up a song. Instead, as he eased his shirt over his flat stomach, he started to hum.

Tula didn't recognize the slow, sultry tune. However, she soon forgot everything except the man in front her as she felt her inner fangirl's heart flutter.

"My own private Fleet Sherman concert. What a privilege."

"Except the paying public doesn't get the *full* show. On stage, I never go further than a bare chest."

Oh, what a chest, Tula sighed with appreciation. Try as she might, she couldn't resist the urge to lick her lips. Part of her wanted to urge Fleet to move faster so she could taste him from top to bottom. The other part—the delayed gratification freak—was happy to let him go at his own pace. Either way, she won.

Thumbs tucked into his waistband, Fleet waggled his eyebrows.

"Ready for the big reveal?"

Honestly, the man was incorrigible.

"Careful, chum," Tula warned. "You've promised me a *big tool*. I would hate to sue for false advertising."

"Nothing false about my equipment."

Tula bit the inside of her cheek to stop from laughing.

"A lot of talk. Where's the action?"

"Don't take my word. Judge for yourself."

In one fluid motion, Fleet whipped off his remaining clothes. And Tula said a silent prayer of thanks for whatever force of nature was responsible for the most stunningly beautiful man she'd ever seen.

In person. In a book. On the wall of a museum. Fleet Sherman put the rest to shame. And all hers.

Tula didn't have the words to tell Fleet how much she wanted him. So, she decided to show him. She slid from the bed to her feet.

"I want to touch you." No one but Fleet could hear, yet she felt the need to whisper.

Fleet raised Tula's hand to his lips. Then placed her palm, still tingling from his kiss, onto his chest.

"Touch to your heart's content."

"My heart's content?" Tula let out a shaky laugh. "We could be here awhile."

"I'm not going anywhere."

Slowly, Tula circled Fleet's tall, strong body. Like a child turned loose in a candy store, she couldn't decide where to start. Her fingers trailed over the side of his waist, across the small of his back and lingered on the slope of his very fine ass. Back where she started, she met Fleet's gaze, a jaunty quip on the tip of her tongue. What she saw made her face flush with shame.

"I'm selfish. I had my fun. Thank you very much." Tula kissed Fleet's clenched jaw. "Are you in pain?"

As Tula moved her hand between his legs, Fleet's head fell back. His breathing ragged, the sound he made was somewhere between a sigh and groan.

"I'll live. Unless you keep teasing." Fleet grabbed Tula's wrist, his hazel eyes flecked with molten gold. "Make up your mind, Tula. Harder. Or not at all."

Fleet's meaning was clear. Playtime was over. Tula had a choice. She could hand the reins back and let Fleet lead, or she could cross the final line and take complete control. The idea was scary. But excitement outweighed fear. By a mile.

Tula placed her hand in the middle of Fleet's chest. And shoved. He landed on his back, arms spread. Eyebrow raised. As if to say, *you have me where you want me. Now what?*

She didn't have to think twice. Without preamble, Tula tossed one, then the other, piece of lace onto the floor. The glint of approval in Fleet's eyes was like a caress to her ego.

"Condom?"

Fleet jerked his head to the side.

"End table drawer."

"Suit up."

Tula didn't have to ask Fleet twice. He caught the foil packet in midair. Before her knees hit the bed, one on each side of his thighs, he was ready for business.

"Ready?"

"I passed ready a long time ago." Fleet placed his hands on Tula's hips as he helped guide her into place. "I'll be lucky if I don't embarrass myself like an untried teenager."

Fleet had nothing to worry about. Tula started out in charge, but Fleet soon took over. He set the pace. Neither of them was in the mood for slow and easy. Wild. Uninhibited. Higher. Higher. Tula didn't think she could take any more.

Then, at the last minute, Fleet reversed their positions. He found her lips with his. Heat. Intense. Tula felt so close. So close. They reached for more. Reached again.

Fleet shouted her name. Tula could only tumble toward earth. Out of control in the best possible way. With Fleet right by her side.

Time passed. Seconds? Minutes? Tula didn't know. The lay sprawled across the bed. Legs tangled. Fleet's chest rose and fell beneath her cheek. She didn't know if all was right with the world. However, in her little corner? Things were right as rain.

"I told you so."

Tula was too comfortable. Too wonderfully languid to summon up a puzzled look. She figured she could manage a question. Barely.

"Remind me. *What* did you tell me?"

"I told you I'd fit."

Tula frowned. What was he talking about? *Oh.* The light dawned. *Fit.* She raised her head and met Fleet's dancing eyes. Always in rhythm, they waited a perfectly placed beat. And burst out laughing.

CHAPTER NINE

"YOU SHOULD COME to Paris."

The second the words were out of Fleet's mouth, he wanted to kick himself. Too soon. Too much. Too... everything. However, the look of excitement in Tula's dark eyes made him toss aside his doubts.

"Paris?" Tula sighed. "I've never been."

Tucked in bed after three marathon sex sessions. After a long, hot, shared shower—and more sex up against the tiled wall—Fleet and Tula lay on their sides facing each other. He didn't look too deep for a reason why he had to touch her. Why he needed the connection when she was only inches away. Fleet simply knew he felt better. Lighter of spirit. Basically happier, when her hand was in his.

Tula snuggled deeper under the covers, her long, damp hair spread out behind her on the pillow. The smell of Fleet's soap on her skin was oddly intimate.

"I'm headed for Dublin at the end of the week. My mother and a friend are off on a world cruise."

"Sounds like fun."

Fleet didn't agree. Trapped on a boat—no matter how big—on the ocean for months? The idea made him shudder. However, the trip was a dream of his mother's for as long as he could remember. The look on her face when he gave her the early Christmas gift had been one of the best and proudest moments of his life.

"Since she won't be home for the holidays, I want to spend some time with her before she sets out to see the world."

Tula smiled. "You're a good son."

"Now and then." Fleet shrugged. "Point is, I'm scheduled to play Paris on the fifteenth. One night only. But we could stay a few extra days. Explore the city. Eat some amazing food."

"Food?" Tula laughed. By now, she knew about his ongoing war with his gluttonous impulses.

"We'll walk everywhere. That way I can indulge. So, what do you say?"

"I'd love to. But…"

As much as Fleet wanted Tula to say yes, he understood her hesitation. Their relationship wasn't clearly defined. He half-expected her to ask his intentions. Where were they going? What would a trip together mean? He should have known better. One of the things he liked about Tula was her refusal to do the expected.

"Consider the invitation open-ended. If you come, great. If not?" Fleet shrugged. "There'll be other times."

"Will there?"

"I hope so," Fleet answered without hesitation.

"I hope so, too."

One hurdle jumped, if not forgotten, they fell into an easy silence.

"Fleet?"

"Hmm?"

"Have you ever met Mick Fleetwood?"

Completely out of the blue, Tula's question was such a surprise, Fleet did something he'd never done before. He confessed the truth.

"We've met. However, Fleet *isn't* short for Fleetwood."

"Your mother wasn't a super fan?"

"Not particularly."

Confused, Tula frowned.

"Why lie?"

"I didn't lie. Exactly." Fleet grew up Catholic. Lies of omission counted as sins in the Church's book. Hardly earthshaking. He'd committed too many sins in his life to worry about one more. "Early in my career, an erroneous rumor buzzed around about the Fleetwood Mac connection. I never confirmed or denied. Nobody has ever seemed interested enough to dig out the truth."

"*When the legend becomes fact, print the legend.*" Tula chuckled. "A quote from *The Man Who Shot Liberty Valance*. My dad's a big John Wayne fan."

"Good line. And close enough." Fleet's lips quirked into a smile. "*If* you drop the legend part."

As confessions went, how Fleet acquired his name wasn't earthshaking. Yet, he had always kept the secret to himself. He shared so much with his fans. With the world.

Fleet had nothing to hide. Which was true. However, even an animal in a zoo had a place all his own. Away from prying eyes. Fleet's name was his metaphorical monkey cage. A little piece of himself nobody else could touch.

Why tell Tula? Because...? Fleet brushed off the question. As with the need to hold her hand, Fleet didn't know. Or rather, he wasn't ready to deal with the implications if he admitted the answer.

"What's the truth? What happened?" Tula prompted.

"Nothing romantic, I'm afraid. The old man was drunk the night I came into the world. Nothing new. He knew my mother had her heart set on the name Finn. He thought Fleet would be a great joke. No rhyme or reason to his choice. Except both start with the same letter."

Eyes bright with emotion, Tula brushed a kiss across the back of his hand.

"Joke's on him. How many women have named their baby after you because they love your music? Dozens? Hundreds?"

All at once, Fleet knew exactly why he'd shared his secret with Tula. Because she was like the sun. Warm. Enveloping. Vital.

Whoa, Fleet thought. *Put the brakes on. Vital? Tula? What the hell was going on?*

"Let's not get carried away." Fleet addressed Tula, but the words were a good reminder for himself.

"Imagine. Little Fleets in every corner of the world," Tula teased, unaware where his thoughts veered. "Quite the tribute."

"I'll give a tribute to imagine."

Fleet slipped under the covers. He couldn't get enough of Tula's beautiful, responsive body. As he moved between her thighs, he left a trail of kisses along her soft skin. His lips curved at Tula's first moaned sigh. And when her hands threaded through his hair, his smile widened.

So good. So right.

Why worry about wayward emotions when sex was so much easier?

FLEET SET THE bowl of grapes on the tray next to a plate of cheese and crackers. Two bottles of water and a half-dozen chocolate cookies he shouldn't, but always seemed to keep in the cupboard, rounded out the varied assortment.

In the bedroom, Tula had grumbled when he left her to put together an impromptu meal. She seemed more interested in sleep than food. Fleet, on the other hand, needed sustenance. His stomach growled, a reminder he'd happily skipped lunch—and dinner—to feast on Tula instead.

As he waited for the kettle to boil, Fleet leaned against the kitchen counter and savored the quiet. As much—perhaps more— than space, he'd longed for a place without the congested city sounds. Or the constant cries of discontented babies. Or loud, angry voices.

Silence was at a premium where Fleet grew up. He chose a job where the music blared. Where a quiet audience was the kiss of death to a singer's career. Fleet loved every second he spent on stage. Thrived on the energy. Poured every bit of his heart and soul into each performance. But away from the filled concert halls and bursting stadiums, he wanted—needed—solitude.

The buzz of Fleet's phone was an unwelcome intrusion. One he couldn't ignore no matter how hard he tried.

"Shit." Fleet grabbed the phone. Sometimes, he hated technology. "Hello?"

"Fleet? This is Smith Carson."

Guilt wasn't an emotion plaguing Fleet's conscience. However, he'd never received a call from his current lover's older brother. While she was asleep, naked, in his bed.

"What time is it?"

What the hell? Fleet's temporary wave of guilt dissipated like a puff of smoke in the face of Smith Carson's question.

"You called me to get the time? Check your phone, asshole."

To his credit, Smith laughed at Fleet's insult.

"I'm in Australia about ready to hit the stage. I guess my internal clock is a bit off."

"And?" He and Smith weren't enemies. But they hardly qualified as chat buddies. "If you have a point, now would be the time to share."

"Impatient jack-off," Smith muttered. "Christmas?"

"Sounds familiar."

"My mother would like you to join us at the farm. If you don't have other plans."

"I..." Blank. Smith's unexpected invitation had knocked every coherent thought from Fleet's brain.

"Mom's big on family. Extended and blood. Since Zoe and I became engaged, we have pretty much inherited the entire Ryder Hart Band. Ryder will be there. Plus Dalton Shaw and Ashe Mathison. And any strays Mom finds between now and then."

Fleet wondered which category he fell under. Since he wasn't family, he must be a stray. He'd been called worse.

"I appreciate the offer, but—"

"A bit of advice? Think awhile before you say no." Smith sighed. "Here's how my mother's mind works. According to Tula, you're an important part of her life. Which, in a roundabout way, makes you family."

"I don't think so."

Family in Fleet's mind consisted of himself and his mother. All the good memories came after he was an adult. The concept of a blissful, boisterous holiday was as foreign to him as a walk on the moon.

"Look, I have to go. Obviously, Tula hasn't asked you yet. When she does, she can fill you in on the particulars."

"Wait," Fleet called out. "About Tula. I didn't think you were exactly thrilled with our partnership."

"The music industry isn't for the faint of heart. As you know."

"I do." Without thinking, Fleet chomped on a cookie.

"I wouldn't have encouraged Tula. However, she has a mind of her own." Smith's sigh sounded long suffering. "I would *love* to put the blame firmly on your shoulders. But you didn't corrupt her away from teaching."

"She's damn talented."

"I know." The pride in Smith's voice was hard to miss. "I want what's best for Tula. And since she assured me you haven't laid a finger on her, I think we *should* get to know each other better."

Talk about a curveball. Fleet hadn't fully processed the idea of Christmas at the Carsons when Smith hit him with *you haven't laid a finger on her.* If Smith had the slightest inkling how Fleet and Tula had occupied their time for the last few hours, he would rescind his invitation in a heartbeat. Then kick Fleet's ass at the soonest possible opportunity.

"I hear my intro music." In the background, Fleet could hear the restless chant of Smith's name. "You have plenty of time to decide. Christmas is almost a month away. I hope you come, Fleet. You'll be welcome."

Quite the dilemma, Fleet thought as he set aside his phone. He'd acquired a fair amount of polish over the years. However, Christmas in Alabama? On a farm? Surrounded by the huge, loving, Carson clan? Most important, with Tula as a witness? The idea scared him shitless.

What if the snot-nosed street urchin he'd never been able to fully exorcise decided to rear his less than socially acceptable head?

Would Tula run if she caught a glimpse of the boy he used to be? Would she see what Fleet feared most? Even the slightest trace of his father's son?

Fleet breathed deeply. No matter how fast he ran, the truth never lagged far behind. *Bad blood.*

You have a choice, Fleet's mother used to tell him. *You can be the man you want to be.* A good man. *A decent man.* Most of the time, he knew she was right. Until—

"Fleet? I started to wonder if you would come back."

Tula wrapped her arms around his waist. Her smile chased away the shadows. Fleet knew he wasn't good enough for her. He knew he would have to give her up. But not now. Not today.

"I was about to make a pot of tea."

"Later."

"How much later?" he asked when he saw her sultry smile.

"As long as it takes."

Fleet let himself sink into her kiss. He couldn't predict the future. The hell with the past. Right now was all he cared about. And he wouldn't squander a single second.

CHAPTER TEN

TULA HIT SEND. Her Ph.D. thesis was on its way to her faculty advisor. If approved, she would present the paper in January, and she would officially be Dr. Petula Joyce Carson.

Quite an accomplishment. If Tula never taught a class, she would always be proud she finished her education. No regrets. With her family's support and the burden of worry behind her, she'd come to realize the value of her education. The maturity and self-confidence she'd gained.

More than a piece of paper, what Tula had learned could never be taken from her. Knowledge equaled power. And out in the real world, power was more valuable than gold.

"All done." Tula snapped closed her laptop. "The next step is out of my hands."

"Your advisor will approve your thesis." Zoe Hart handed Tula a cup of coffee.

"Probably." Tula wasn't worried. However, nothing was ever certain. "What makes you so sure?"

"I read the paper." Zoe's blue eyes twinkled. "Not that I understood everything. I never stepped foot on a college campus. Except to play a concert."

"Oh, please," Tula groaned. "You know more about everything than any person I know."

Zoe started touring with *The Ryder Hart Band* when she was eighteen. She occupied her time on buses and planes, filling her brain with a mind-boggling variety of information. Proof a well-rounded education didn't always come from a classroom.

"Your paper is brilliant, Tula." Zoe dropped her awe-shucks façade. "Are you going to insist we call you Dr. Carson?"

"What do you think?"

"I think you'd be crazy not to."

"We'll see. I imagine the novelty will wear off." Tula laughed. "In ten or twenty years."

Cup in hand, Tula moved to the bank of windows. Los Angeles stretched out before her, blanketed by a hazy December sky. Tired of her own company, she'd spent the last two days with Zoe and Smith.

"Are you finally ready to tell me why you decided to visit?"

Tula glanced over her shoulder. Zoe's gaze was steady, and understanding. And to think when they first met, she thought the world-famous rock star was a bit on the cold side. Time had taught her the truth was just the opposite. Zoe didn't open her heart easily, but when she cared, her loyalty and love were unshakable.

"I'd hoped a different view might help clarify my thoughts. I was wrong. I'm just as confused—maybe more so—than I was when I arrived."

Zoe joined her. Shoulder to shoulder, they sipped their coffee.

"Problems never stay where you want them. I know. Your brother had a way of popping up in my head no matter how many miles physically separated us. What's going on with Fleet Sherman?"

"I made my move."

"Good for you." Zoe tapped her cup against Tula's. "Fleet's never struck me as a fool. I assume he was smart enough to say yes?"

"I went to Fleet's house in Vermont so we could work."

"And…?" Tula flushed at the memory. Zoe let out a knowing chuckle. "I assume you didn't get a lot of writing done."

"No." Tula hugged the memory of her time with Fleet close. "He was wonderful. Beyond my fantasies. He probably ruined me for any other man."

"Sounds promising. But?"

"Something changed. I can't explain what. Fleet was there, but he wasn't." Tula had tried to pinpoint the moment he started to pull away. "I think he was sorry he asked me to join him in Paris."

Tula left out the intimate parts of the story. What happened and was said between lovers was nobody else's business. However, the basics were enough to give Zoe a clear picture of the situation.

"Did Fleet take back his invitation?"

"No." However, just before she left, Tula mentioned the trip again. "I told Fleet I'd let him know if I could go. He didn't seem to care one way or the other."

"What did Fleet say when you invited him to the farm for Christmas?"

"I didn't invite him." Tula meant to, but the timing never seemed right. "I know Mom wants to meet him, but I don't think Fleet is ready for the entire Carson clan. I was afraid he might feel pressured."

"Oh, boy." Eyes closed, Zoe's head fell forward. "Smith called Fleet."

"Why?" Tula wasn't sure she wanted to know.

"To ask him to come for Christmas. And before you think Smith poked his nose into your business, the call wasn't his idea."

"Mom," Tula sighed.

Zoe nodded. "She thought an invitation from Smith—added to yours—would make Fleet feel welcome. Like the entire family was in favor of his visit."

"Except I dropped the ball."

Tula could imagine what must have gone through Fleet's head. He was good enough for Tula to sleep with, but not good enough to spend Christmas with her and the Carson clan.

"Fleet is the most confident man I've ever met. Except where family is concerned." The coffee in Tula's stomach threatened to come back up. "I screwed up."

"Maybe a little. But your intentions were good." Zoe placed a comforting arm around Tula's waist. "Give Fleet a call. He'll understand."

"I have to talk to him in person." No time for second thoughts, Tula handed Zoe her cup. "I have to go to Paris."

"I'll make the arrangements. Transatlantic flights are always better in a private jet."

For once, Tula didn't argue. The prideful need to pay her own way be damned. She wanted to get to Fleet as fast as possible.

"If I have to travel in the lap of luxury, I guess I'll survive."

Hopefully, Fleet would listen with an open mind. Already on the phone, Zoe winked. All at once, Tula felt better. She knew what she had to say. What she had to do. And with the best lead guitar player in the world on her side, how could she fail?

ZOE WASN'T JUST on Tula's side. She was a miracle worker.

While Tula worried about little details about how she would get to Alabama, pack a bag, and somehow get to Paris before the start of Fleet's concert, Zoe pushed Tula's concerns away with a wave of her hand.

An hour after the decision was made, Tula was on *The Ryder Hart Band's* private jet, winging her way to the City of Lights. In what seemed like a blink, she was seated in a jam-packed concert hall. All courtesy of Zoe Hart.

"A car and driver will pick you up at the airport." Zoe had filled Tula in as she hustled her into a waiting taxi. "Don't worry about what you'll wear. Clothes. Shoes. Everything you need will be at the hotel, in the room booked for you. The concierge will have your ticket to the show—third-row center. And a backstage pass for after."

"How?" Head spinning, Tula hugged Zoe goodbye.

"I have the best designers in the world on speed dial." Naturally, Tula thought. "As for the rest? I called in a few favors. Merry Christmas a little early."

"The gift I bought for you doesn't even compare."

Zoe hugged her one more time. "If you're happy, we're more than even."

Happy didn't begin to describe Tula's emotions. She smoothed her hand over the crushed velvet of her form-hugging, winter-white leggings. The knee-high boots in almost the exact same color and cropped leather bomber jacket in a perfectly contrasting sable-brown fit like they were made for her. Knowing Zoe, maybe they were. Either way, the outfit was exactly what Tula needed to boost her confidence and settle her nerves.

"Lucky thirteen."

A young woman around Tula's age shouted above the increasingly restless crowd. Bright-blue hair spiked in various directions. Torn jean jacket. Torn jeans. Motorcycle boots decorated with a dozen looped chains. A little more punk than rock. But if her beaming smile were any indication, she was right where she wanted to be.

"Pardon me?" Tula shouted back.

"Tonight is my thirteenth Fleet Sherman concert. I have five more scheduled for next year."

"Wow." Tula was impressed.

"The man speaks to me, you know? Right down to my soul. My name is Bridgette, by the way."

"Tula."

"Cool." Bridgette chomped on a wad of gum. "What's your number?"

"My number?" Tula frowned. Oh. Her *number*. "I'm a first timer."

"No kidding. Hey, Jimmy. We got ourselves a Fleet virgin."

Tula coughed. Then chuckled. Then out and out laughed her ass off. A Fleet virgin. If Bridgette only knew.

"TEN MINUTES, MR. Sherman."

Fleet rubbed his temples and for the first time in his career, wished he was any place but here. A warm, sandy beach. A snowy mountaintop. Hell, he'd settle for an all-night Denny's in Craphole, USA. He'd seen enough of them in his early touring days. One more wouldn't matter.

Fleet didn't care. As long as he didn't have to set foot on stage.

Because he didn't feel low enough, Fleet picked up the telegram he found waiting in his dressing room when he arrived.

Who the hell sends telegrams anymore?

The *Dublin Metropolitan Police*, that's who. And why the message came directly to Fleet instead of his team of high-priced lawyers, he didn't know. Heads would roll over the fiasco.

"And asses will be kicked."

"Tell me who's on your shit list. I'll take care of the problem."

Fleet didn't respond to his manager's request. Without turning, he crumpled the paper into a ball.

"Showtime, Roni." Fleet tossed the telegram into the wastepaper basket. "Did you need something?"

"I need to know what crawled up your ass." Roni held up two leather jackets. One black. One navy blue. Fleet grabbed the black. "Are your panties still in a twist over Tula Carson?"

In a moment of sheer idiocy, Fleet mentioned he'd invited Tula to Paris. And regretted the slip ever since.

"You're getting close to the line, Roni. Do us both a favor and don't cross over."

"Fine." Roni held up her hands in defeat. "I thought you might like to know she's in the audience. But—"

Halfway out the dressing room door, Fleet froze.

"Tula's here?"

"Zoe Carson called to ask for a ticket." Roni sighed. "I thought you'd be happy."

"A ticket for Tula?" Well, shit.

"And a backstage pass." Impatient, Roni crossed her arms. "I can cancel the pass if you don't want to see her."

Fleet knew what he had to do. The truth didn't make him happy. Hell, he didn't expect to be happy for a very long time. However, for Tula's sake, he didn't have a choice.

"Don't cancel."

Grim, Fleet headed toward the stage. He *had* to see Tula. But after tonight, she'd never want to see him again.

CHAPTER ELEVEN

WHEN THE LIGHTS came up, the people around Tula seemed energized. Non-stop, raucous, high-voltage Fleet Sherman from beginning to end, she had the feeling the buzzing crowd would have gladly worshiped at the rock god's feet all night.

Tula was right with them. When Fleet had first taken the stage, she felt something was off. From where she stood, she thought she saw something in his eyes. Anger? Resignation? A second later, his gaze cleared and she chalked the moment to the lights and her imagination.

Two and a half hours later, Tula could unequivocally declare her first Fleet Sherman concert experience a complete success.

Something had seemed off. Different. Though she hadn't seen Fleet perform in person until tonight, she'd watched videos. Downloaded concerts. When she took her seat, she was sure she knew what to expect.

And Fleet delivered. He owned the stage. And the audience. They were with him from the first note to the last. Dynamic. Charismatic. Sweat dripped from every inch of his body.

When Fleet wiped his bare chest, Bridgette leaned close and shouted, "I'd give my last dime to trade places with that towel."

Tula would have bet *her* last dime Bridgette wasn't alone. Fleet gave his all to his fans. And they walked away happy.

"Hey." Bridgette laid a hand on Tula's arm. "We're going to keep this party moving at a club across town. Want to come?"

With a shake of her head, Tula smiled as she thought of the backstage pass tucked safely in her purse.

"Thanks. But I have other plans."

Big plans. Exciting plans. Hopeful plans. Tula made her way against the throng. She wasn't in a hurry—good thing. Most people were anxious to exit. But enough were determined to linger. Either to chat with friends and fellow concert-goers. Or the usual groupies who lived in hope they would get backstage and catch the eye of a band member. Maybe even the great Fleet Sherman himself.

Good luck, ladies, Tula thought as she wiggled by. Honestly, she wished them only the best. Another time. A different rock star. But not Fleet. Not tonight.

If Tula had her way? Not ever.

A large, tattooed man with a shaved head and the biggest hands Tula had ever seen, blocked the stage door. A black t-shirt with Fleet's face and logo stenciled on the front stretched across his muscular chest. When she approached, he crossed his arms, shaking his head before she could speak.

"Sorry, honey. The exits are in the other direction."

"But—"

"Concert's over. Time to leave."

Tula had to admit the man seemed well suited for his chosen profession. Forceful. Dedicated. However, if his career in security ever fell through, he could always find work as a stand-in for mid-sized mountain range.

Smiling. Only mildly intimidated, Tula handed the man her pass.

"All-access, I believe."

Diligent, he checked the paper up, down, and sideways.

"Can't be too careful," he said as he opened the door. "You wouldn't believe what some fans will do to get by me."

Tula could guess—she had a vivid imagination. However, she really didn't want to know the details. Some things were better left unsaid.

The energy backstage was different after a concert. Before was all anticipation and nerves. After, the desire to wrap things up with brutal efficiency and get the hell out of Dodge.

"Ms. Carson?" A woman in head-to-toe black greeted Tula with an outstretched hand. "I'm Roni McKay. Nice to meet you. Follow me."

Fleet's manager wasn't big in stature. However, from the keen glint in her dark eyes and gruff attitude, Tula had the feeling the woman could bulldoze her way over the biggest obstacle without breaking a sweat. Or one of her perfectly manicured nails.

"Thanks for everything." Tula zigged and zagged around stacks of equipment. "The ticket couldn't have been easy to come by at the last minute."

"Zoe Hart is a hard woman to turn down. Besides, Fleet asked you to come. Right?"

"He did. But..." Tula didn't know how to explain. So she didn't. "Does Fleet know I'm here?"

Roni hesitated. She looked at Tula as if she wanted to elaborate. She shrugged and the moment passed.

"Zoe said you wanted to surprise him." Roni stopped at the end of a long, narrow hallway. She nodded toward the door. "Go on in."

The day had been a huge whirlwind. Even on the flight to Paris, Tula hadn't given herself a chance to stop and think. To ask if? Now—with only a piece of wood between them—she hesitated. She glanced around, but Roni was nowhere to be seen. She was on her own.

Taking a deep breath, Tula raised her hand and gave the door two quick raps.

"Come on in."

Tula had a choice. She could make a tentative entrance. Or she could be brave. Throw the door open with a bold, *here I am*, confidence.

"The new Tula," she reminded herself.

Shoulders back, Tula turned the knob. A smile on her lips, heart pounding, she stepped into the dressing room. And what she found was like a fist to her gut.

Bare chested, still dressed in his stage clothes, Fleet lay sprawled on a long, black sofa. Sprawled across Fleet, three half-dressed women. Fleet petted the buxom blonde as if she were a favored pet. And the woman purred.

"Tula? Glad to see ya, darlin'."

Tula's legs felt like half-set Jell-O left out in the mid-day sun. Locked knees and pride were the only things keeping her upright. Plus the overwhelming desire to shove Fleet Sherman's suddenly thick as molasses brogue back down his throat.

"I didn't realize you were occupied." Tula's voice was steady and unnaturally neutral.

"Nothing unusual. Just a little after-show fun."

Who are you? Tula wanted to yell. *What have you done with my Fleet Sherman?* But she kept her questions to herself, afraid she wouldn't like his answers.

"What are you doing way over there?" Fleet patted the sofa. "Plenty of room. Come and join us."

Tragedy or farce. Tula wouldn't stick around to find out. Before she broke into a million pieces in front of Fleet's eyes, she turned and walked out the way she came. She would run, but Roni McKay blocked Tula's path.

"Please don't go."

"They're laughing." Tula couldn't believe her ears. However, the sound of high-pitched giggles was unmistakable. Anger mixed with misery and humiliation. Fist clenched, she turned on Roni. "When you sent me in there, did you know what I'd find? Are you his pimp as well as his manager?"

"You need to jab at me?" With surprising strength, Roni stopped Tula's attempt to pull away. "I'll take the hit. Once. But you need to hear me out."

"Why? Give me one good reason I shouldn't knock you on your ass and get out of here."

"Because the man behind that door isn't the real Fleet Sherman."

An hour ago, Tula would have agreed. If someone had tried to warn her? She wouldn't have listened. But now? Her vision was perfect. As much as she wished she could deny the truth, she had to believe her own eyes.

"Fleet didn't make me any promises. I don't have the right to judge him."

Except Tula had been so sure he cared for her. Maybe his feelings weren't as strong as hers. But where was the kind, respectful man she thought she knew?

"I can't think of much I wouldn't do for Fleet." Roni sighed. "Including put my job on the line. I'm pretty good at reading people. So, for everyone involved, don't prove me wrong. Here."

Not sure what difference a crumpled piece of paper could make, Tula reluctantly scanned the contents. As she read, she felt her anger fade. For clarity, she read the lines again before she lifted her eyes and met Roni's worried gaze.

"When did the telegram arrive?"

"Before Fleet went on. If I'd had any idea, I wouldn't have let him see the damn thing. Fucking royal cock-up." Roni's grip on Tula's arms loosened, but she didn't let go. "Fleet doesn't talk about his childhood. But I can tell by your expression he told you. At least a bit."

"Fleet told me everything."

Surprise flashed in Roni's eyes. Relief followed.

"So, you understand?"

"I think so. Maybe."

"Please, tell me you won't leave. Fleet needs—"

"A good kick in the ass."

Roni snorted. "Probably." When Tula raised an eyebrow, Roni relented. "Definitely. However, his actions weren't malicious."

"No." Tula nodded. "Foolish. Wrongheaded. But not malicious."

"You're going back in?" Roni didn't wait for an answer. Fleet's manager rushed to open the dressing room door as if she was afraid Tula might change her mind. "Good luck."

"Thanks."

If Tula found Fleet in the mid-orgy, she'd turn heel, leave, and she'd try for the rest of her life to pretend she didn't care. Good luck.

Since Tula was almost positive Fleet's goal hadn't been sex with his groupies, she figured she didn't need to shield her eyes from a potential *Sodom and Gomorrah* situation.

"I didn't know what to expect. But cards? Really?"

The pouting three buxom babes were in the middle of what appeared to be *Go Fish*. Tula didn't know if the choice of the game had to do with their level of maturity or intelligence.

Fleet sat on the other side of the room. In his hand, an unopened bottle of champagne. He never drank. Tula planned to make certain tonight wasn't the night he started.

"Put down the bottle and tell your little friends good night. We need to talk."

"Do we now?" Absently, Fleet peeled the foil off the cork. "Whatever you have to say, my little friends can hear."

As if to illustrate the absurdity of the gathering, one of the women stuck her tongue out—at Tula.

Tula held up the telegram. Fleet's gaze jerked toward the empty trash can.

"Roni." Fleet ground his manager's name out through gritted teeth. "She'll be looking for a job in the morning."

"No. She won't. Because by morning, you'll have stopped with the pity party long enough to realize how lucky you are to have her."

Fleet grunted.

"You should go, Tula."

"We're going to talk. Now. If you don't want the world to know your business?" Tula nodded toward the three fascinated eavesdroppers. "Ask them to leave, Fleet."

"Go."

"But, Fleet." The pretty redhead somehow managed to speak, whine, and bite her bottom lip all at once. "We'll give you a lot more pleasure than she can."

"Fun's over, ladies." Fleet rolled to his feet. He opened the door and ushered the protesting women from the room. "Roni?"

Roni had jumped to her feet from a nearby chair.

"Fleet. I—"

"Have my driver drop these ladies wherever they want to go."

"Of course. Fleet…"

"Later, Roni."

"Are we okay?"

"Probably." Fleet sighed. "I'll decide tomorrow. Or the next day."

Fleet closed the door on Roni's hopeful expression. He didn't turn. Or glance Tula's way. Back to her, he rested one hand on the door, the other he used to rub his face.

"You have your wish. We're alone. Apparently, you feel the need to rip me a new one." Fleet rotated his shoulders as if in anticipation. "Have at it."

Anger and hurt washed away as Tula's heart constricted. Fleet's pain was a living thing. Palpable. She didn't want to argue or berate. All she wanted was to take away his hurt.

Tula crossed the distance between them. Her outstretched hand hovered over Fleet's back. Without touching, she could feel the tension radiate from his bunched muscles. As Tula eased an arm around his waist, he stiffened.

"Tula..."

"Shh," Tula coaxed with a kiss to Fleet's bare skin.

Cheek pressed to his back, Tula completed the hug, her arms wrapped around him. The flesh of Fleet's flat stomach quivered beneath her palms as he let out a long, ragged stream of air.

They stood without speaking. Their thoughts private. Slowly, Fleet's rigid stance relaxed. Not completely. Just enough to let them both breathe a little easier.

"I deserve your wrath." Fleet squeezed Tula's hand before he moved from her embrace. "Say whatever you need. I won't fly into a rage. Or fall apart. Seems you have the magic touch." A half smile formed on his lips. "A fact I already knew."

Honestly, Tula didn't have a plan when she entered Fleet's dressing room for the second time. She talked a big game, but Fleet's ass was safe. She'd never struck—or kicked—another person in her life, and had no plans to start.

"I *should* be angry," Tula said as she gathered her thoughts. "I am angry. However…"

"Go on." Fleet leaned a hip against the dressing table, his hands rested on the surface. Tula couldn't detect any sparks of color in the depths of his hazel eyes. They were too dulled with resignation.

"Truth is, I'm more disappointed than anything else. I know we haven't known each other long. But I thought we'd made a connection. Strong. Getting stronger all the time. I guess I was wrong."

"I guess you were."

"Bullshit." Tula saw red. "Congratulations. Mad just replaced disappointed. I'm your friend, Fleet. And your lover."

Seemingly unconcerned, Fleet simply shrugged.

Great. Tula raised her eyes to the ceiling. If anger and sentimentality wouldn't crack his melancholy, she'd deal in facts.

"Groupies? Really. If you wanted to chase me away, you should have thought of something more original."

"I didn't have a lot of time to think out a plan."

"Obviously."

"You should have left, Tula. I don't have anything to give you except trouble."

Tula glanced at the paper clutched in her grip. Fleet's kryptonite. No! She had to make him understand. He wasn't anything like the man who sired him.

"What could you have done if you'd known your father had been released on bail?"

Fleet's fingers tightened their grip on the table's edge, but his expression remained calm as the surface of a mountain lake.

"Tracked the dog down and put us both out of our misery."

Tula didn't believe Fleet was capable of murder. To protect someone he loved in the heat of the moment? Yes. But he could never kill with cool, thought-out malice.

"And you'd end up in prison. One Carson exchanged for another."

Fleet's lips quirked. "Blood will tell."

"When was the last time you trashed a house? Tell me when you punched a defenseless woman—multiple times—before you tried to rape her?"

Tula cursed the telegram and the graphic details the Dublin police should have kept to themselves.

"The woman shouldn't have been there." Fleet's eyes carried a far-off look.

Silently, Tula urged Fleet to keep talking. When he paused, she gave him a prompt.

"The house belongs to your mother?"

"Aye. Near the edge of the city. She always dreamed of a sweet little cottage all her own. Roses in front. A garden in the back. My scumbag father tore out every bush. Hacked up every shrub and flower."

Tula frowned. The telegram had been filled with outrageously graphically specific information for such an impersonal form of communication. However, she hadn't read anything specific about the damage to the cottage.

"How do you know about the roses?"

"Made a call or two. I still have a few close friends who keep their ears to the ground." Fleet rubbed the back of his neck. "Seven years without a free breath in his lungs and what's the first thing he does? Goes after his ex-wife. A week earlier and he would have found her."

118

"The woman in your mother's house?"

"Mrs. Finney. She and her husband agreed to watch the place for my mother. Bad timing. She dropped by to give the house a quick check and water the house plants."

"She found your father."

"He fell asleep. Can you imagine? When he didn't find anybody home, he trashed the inside. Then curled up on the sofa like he didn't have a care in the world. Knowing the way his mind works, I doubt if he did."

Tula knew the rest. Mrs. Finney arrived early the next morning. She was distressed by the damage to the roses, but she assumed some local kids did the damage. She entered the house, had just dialed the police to make a report when Mick Sherman attacked her.

"The open phone line is what saved her. The officer on the other end heard Mrs. Finney's scream. He sent a car around to investigate."

"He didn't rape her."

"Not for want of trying. But you're right. The police arrived before the bastard could do his worst. Mrs. Finney is in the hospital with a broken jaw. Some comfort. She could be dead."

"You arranged to pay her medical bills." Tula didn't have to ask. She knew the good inside Fleet even if he didn't.

"I have the money. No pain in tossing a bit around to salve my conscience."

"You aren't your father, Fleet." Frustrated, she grabbed him and gave him a shake. "You have no reason to feel guilty."

"Yet, I do."

Tula knew an opening when she heard one.

"One more way you differ from Mick Sherman." Tula smoothed her hands up and down Fleet's arms. "He's back behind bars. Thank the Lord. But do you think he's racked with regret?"

"No. The bastard always finds a way to hang the blame on somebody else."

Tula dipped her head until she could look into Fleet's eyes.

"I understand the shock when you found out what he did. But you aren't responsible. You aren't him."

For a second, she thought Fleet meant to touch her. *Please, please, touch me.* Instead, he eased away until several feet separated them.

"I'm not boyfriend material. And before you protest, we both know where you hoped we were headed."

"And you?" Tula wouldn't let him rewrite history. "You have to admit you felt the same."

"I learned a long time ago I don't always get what I want. Besides, you must have changed your mind."

"Why?"

"The invitation to spend Christmas with your family?"

Fleet sounded so defeated Tula felt her heart crack. Not break. Not yet.

"Oh." With all the drama, Tula had forgotten the original reason she'd come to Paris.

"Oh, indeed."

Fleet tried to turn away, but Tula refused to let him turn the crack in her heart into a permanent break. Not without a fight.

"We were barely lovers, Fleet. As much as I wanted to ask? And I did. More than you'll ever know. I was afraid you'd think I had designs on you."

"Designs?" Fleet shrugged. "Maybe I would have. We'll never know. Which is for the best."

Tula's pulse raced. She placed Fleet's hand over her chest, certain he could feel the pounding beat. "I'm yours, Fleet. All you have to do is take a chance. Your *bad blood* isn't standing in our way. You are."

"For once in my adult life, I want to do something selfless. Help me, Tula. *Let* me do the right thing."

What could she say? Tula didn't have the words to change Fleet's mind. To convince him he was wrong. About himself. About them. About everything. He wanted her to walk away? Fine. But she wouldn't go without one more memory.

"Kiss me goodbye."

Fleet rested his forehead against hers. As if he couldn't help himself, he cupped Tula's cheek.

"Not a good idea."

"Please?"

"See?" Fleet sighed, his eyes on her lips. "When I really want something, good intentions fly out the window."

Tula sank into the kiss. Unable to get enough, she pressed herself close, closer. Her fingers gripped Fleet's waist, caressed his back. Smooth and hot. Supple.

"Tula. We can't." Fleet stopped Tula's hands when she started to unbuckle his belt. "A kiss is one thing. But... A man can only take so much."

"A woman's no different. Not really." Tula kissed Fleet's chest. "You're about to send me away. I'll never again touch you. Feel your body rise above me. Look in your eyes as we become one. I'll never forgive myself if I leave without being with you one last time."

"You're a witch." Fleet dropped his hands from hers. "Have your way. If you must."

Tula chuckled. "Poor Fleet. If the idea of sex with me is so repugnant, I give you permission to lie back and think of England."

"Ireland, darlin'. Always Ireland. However," Fleet slid Tula's jacket from her shoulders. "I think I can stir up enough interest for full participation."

Clothes melted away, along with the last of Fleet's reticence. He was with Tula every step, every touch, and caress, every sigh. Words, always so important when they were together, weren't necessary. They were intent on remembering.

Slowly—there was no need to hurry—Fleet joined their bodies. If Tula couldn't verbally express her feelings, she let them shine in her eyes. *Love*. She knew her heart. She loved Fleet Sherman. And she would never be afraid or ashamed of the emotion.

The end came too soon. Tula would have happily stayed in his arms forever. However, Fleet had reached his limit. He stood, gathered her clothes, and handed them to her.

"Ready to go?" Fleet asked after he dressed.

"Almost." Tula tugged on her boot. All she had left was her jacket.

"Let me."

Fleet held the jacket, lifting Tula's hair out of the way. Before he moved away, he placed a kiss on the top of her head. The gesture, so sweet and natural, put another crack in Tula's already fragile heart.

"I'll call you a ride."

"No need." Tula texted her driver. "My car is outside waiting for me."

"I'll walk you out."

Couldn't they say goodbye here and now? But when Fleet held out his hand, she only hesitated for a second. His gesture somehow felt right. If not the perfect ending, as close as they would get.

Together, fingers entwined, they made their way through the near-deserted building. Fleet waved off the driver. He opened the door himself.

"Goodbye, Tula."

"Goodbye."

In the car, Tula didn't cry. Instead, she sat back, hands folded in her lap, and quietly waited for her heart to crumble into a million pieces.

CHAPTER TWELVE

SNOW IN LATE December wasn't a rare occurrence on the Carson farm.

True, snowfall tended toward the thin and wispy. More often than not, the flakes melted as soon as they hit the ground.

However, every few years, they were treated to the joy and wonder of a real, honest to goodness, white Christmas.

"Remind me again why I'm the one with a shovel in my hands?" Smith grumbled as he scooped another section of snow from the walkway.

On the porch, watching without an ounce of sympathy, Ryder Hart, Dalton Shaw, and Ashe Mathison exchanged grins. Since Smith and Zoe's engagement, *The Ryder Hart Band* and their ladies had become treasured members of the Carson clan. They spent much of their free time on the farm and were as welcome as any blood relative.

The band's presence was expected—practically mandatory— for all holidays and special occasions. Naturally, Christmas was no exception.

With a shrug, Ryder leaned against the railing, his arms crossed over his stylish navy pea coat.

"You drew the short straw."

"I wasn't in the room. How could I draw a straw or anything else?"

"We knew you wouldn't want us to leave you out of the fun," Dalton chimed in. His blue eyes glinted with good humor. "I picked for you."

"By proxy," Ashe said before Smith could argue. "All above board."

From where she sat on the porch swing her father built, Tula listened with affection as the men argued like brothers. Which, for all intents and purposes, they were.

Smith was a new addition to the close-knit group. At first, they tolerated each other for Zoe's sake. Now? Their bond was tight. Friends. And yes, brothers.

"You could help." Smith rotated his shoulders. The snow was only a few inches deep, but the walkway was long and winding. "I know for a fact there are at least two more shovels in the tool shed."

"We'd love to help. Really." Dalton winked at Tula as he and Ashe clicked mugs of steaming mulled cider. "But you're almost done. We'd hate to take away your sense of accomplishment over a job well done."

"Assholes."

"Hey. Watch the language." Zoe Hart admonished as she joined her brother and bandmates. Two equally beautiful, yet unquestionably unique women trailed behind. "Around here, children pop up in the oddest places and at the oddest times."

"I swear three more hatched when I wasn't looking." Colleen McNamara, gorgeous and curvy as always, placed an arm around Dalton's waist. Her fiancé, besotted beyond belief, kissed her cheek.

Belle Richards, the love of Ashe's life, smiled as he wrapped her in a warm hug.

"I think I'd like a little rugrat or two." Belle's smile turned into a grin when Ashe choked on his cider. "Relax. My biological clock hasn't kicked into gear. One day. In the future. But not anytime soon."

As Tula watched, envy—unwelcome and shameful—covered the surface of her skin. Like thousands of tiny, painful pinpricks. And like her broken heart, she knew she wouldn't die from the wounds.

But Tula suffered. Oh, how she suffered.

Tula adored her extended family. Every single one of them. However, at the moment, she wished they weren't quite so happy. A shared misery would give her some relief. A balm to her tattered soul.

Zoe blew a kiss of encouragement at Smith before she walked across the porch to join Tula.

"How are you feeling?"

"Lousy."

"A step up from desolate." Zoe gave Tula's hand a sympathetic pat. "Would you feel better if I arranged to give Fleet a good old-fashioned ass whipping? Or is the word whooping? I'm still not fluent in Alabamian."

Tula could smile because she knew Zoe wasn't serious enough to follow through. Though she appreciated the thought.

"Whooping. However, the word isn't exclusive to my home state."

"If you say so." Zoe returned Tula's smile, but the concern didn't leave her eyes.

Zoe had become Tula's confidant. The one person who knew every twist and turn of her brief, ill-fated love affair. She tried her best to stay upbeat around everyone else. With Zoe, Tula could relax and simply feel miserable.

"Love is in the air." Zoe nodded toward their perfectly paired-off friends. "Sorry."

"If you have to apologize because you're happy, I've moved beyond sad, and I'm sliding fast toward pathetic."

Tula gazed toward the barnyard and the snow-laden wooden fence. So peaceful. So beautiful. She needed to remember how lucky she was to have a warm and welcoming place to come to. She needed to count her blessings—her family and good health at the top of the list.

"I won't tell you things will get better." Zoe's lips curved slightly as she shrugged.

"I'll get to a point where I don't think about Fleet every other second." Every second was more accurate. "I can't even listen to the radio for a distraction."

"Too much Fleet music?"

"The man is *way* too popular for my own good. Tomorrow's Christmas Eve." Tula rested her head on Zoe's shoulder when her friend hugged her close. "I know I shouldn't wish the holiday away."

"Go ahead. I promise not to tell."

Tula was lucky, she reminded herself once more. She had so much, she would be greedy to wish for what she couldn't have. Yet, the human heart wasn't always the most rational of organs. She wanted Fleet. Here. Now.

And Tula feared, forever.

"HAPPY DAY BEFORE the day before Christmas, my love."

"Same to you, beautiful lady."

The sound of his mother's laughter lightened Fleet's mood. Not a lot. However, he'd lived the last few days in a pitch-black haze. So, anything was an improvement.

"Where are you?"

The picture on Fleet's phone moved from Fiona Sherman's smiling face to a sun-drenched, glistening body of water. Boats bobbed, their sails in various stages of readiness.

"Greece. Loutro, to be exact. While the cruise ship is docked, some of us decided to take a tour of several fishing villages."

"You're having a good time."

"I am."

Fleet could hear the carefree happiness in his mother's voice and knew he'd made the right decision not to tell her what happened in Dublin. Mrs. Finney was on the mend, her family around her for support. Repairs would start on the cottage after the first of the year and would be done long before Fiona returned.

As for Mick Sherman. He wouldn't be raising a fist to anyone but his fellow prison mates for a long, long time.

Expression neutral, Fleet's hand balled into a fist. He wasn't over the anger. He wasn't sure he ever would be. Another reason he was better off alone, far, far away from Tula.

"I met someone."

Fiona's out-of-the-blue announcement made Fleet blink several times, certain he must have misheard.

"I imagine you've met several dozen *someones*."

"Don't be deliberately dense, Fleet. His name is Denis O'Shaughnessy. And yes. He's Irish. Dublin born. Though he lives in London. A fact I've decided to forgive him for."

"Are we talking holiday romance or something more?" The son in Fleet wasn't certain how he felt about either.

"We'll see. Early days."

Fiona fluffed the ends of her stylish bob. Not born a blonde, she'd recently embraced the honey color wholeheartedly. Slender, the worn creases Fleet remembered from his youth had faded from her face. A woman in her fifties who once looked and acted ten years older, she walked and talked with a youthful vigor.

"Enough about me. Tell me about your Tula."

"Damn, Roni," Fleet muttered.

"She was right to call." A shadow entered Fiona's eyes. "Look at me, Fleet. I've finally let go of the past. I don't simply exist. I'm living. You need to do the same."

"I have a good life. Enviable, some might say."

Fleet couldn't miss the defensive tone in his voice. Neither could his mother.

"I'm so proud of the man you've become, Fleet. I always hoped when you met the right woman, you'd realize money and fame aren't enough."

"I don't need a woman in my life to be happy."

"True." Fiona nodded. "You've had plenty of women. What you need is the *right* one. Roni seems to think Tula Carson qualifies."

Fleet opened his mouth to argue. To curse Roni. To deny his feeling. Feelings which were nobody else's business. But why bother. His mother would know the words were a lie.

"Tula is beautiful. And smart. And funny. And the kindest person I've ever met. She's…"

"Everything? Oh, my sweet boy. Tula must be special indeed." Fiona's eyes glistened as she sighed, her hands clutched to her heart. "You're in love."

A fact Fleet already figured out for himself.

"I'd be selfish to tell her."

"You'd be selfish not to."

Fleet scoffed. "How do you figure?

"I can't think of a more precious gift than to love someone." Fiona smiled. "Except to have someone—the *right* someone—love you in return."

Fleet's heart constricted. Since the moment he closed the door of Tula's car, he'd lived with a litany of doubts. He wanted her. Wanted to go to her. However, when he started to waffle, he reminded himself of all the reasons why his decision to end things had been for the best. Each day. Each hour. Each minute. The reasons grew fewer and fewer. Harder and harder to remember. Until only one question remained.

"I don't know if I'm right for her."

"Something tells me Tula knows. She'll make the right choice. For both of you."

A sliver of hope could be a glorious thing. Or an eternal, raging slice of hell. Fleet was balanced in the middle, uncertain which way he would fall.

"Take a chance, Fleet. Something tells me you'll make Tula's Christmas a whole lot brighter if you do."

"What if she doesn't love me?"

"Not love Fleet Sherman?" Fiona gasped as if the idea was unthinkable. "If your Tula is as smart as you claim, her heart is yours for the taking."

Unless Tula had come to her senses.

"I have to go." Apparently, Fiona felt she'd pushed as far as she could. "I love you. Always. No matter what."

"I love you, too. Enjoy yourself." Genuinely happy for his mother, Fleet winked. "And your new beau."

A girlish blush on her cheeks, Fiona blew Fleet a kiss before the screen went black.

On the sofa in his living room, Fleet picked up his guitar and strummed a few chords. He wanted to rock. Something with a pulse-pounding, forget his troubles beat.

Unfortunately, his fingers refused to cooperate.

One tune filled his heart. The one he'd come to think of as Tula's song. The rhythm, the mood, drew him in. Swirled like a velvet vise around his heart. Slowly, but inexorably. Sexy, but not overtly so. A subtle sensuality.

Exactly like Tula.

Fleet had tried. He'd done his best. However, he couldn't chase the melody from his head. Any more than he could expel the woman from his soul. Sometimes a man couldn't fight the inevitable. Sometimes, he should stop trying.

Snow fell outside his window, the blanket of white was another reminder of how alone he felt. How his home, always a sanctuary from the outside world, had turned into a self-imposed prison.

Eyes closed, Fleet let the music flow. Note by note, he felt the chains that bound him for so long, fall to the ground.

CHAPTER THIRTEEN

TULA WALKED THROUGH the newly fallen snow. She stopped at the top of the hill overlooking the farm and breathed in the crisp air. She dug her chilled hands into the pockets of her long, winter coat. Served her right. She'd been in such a hurry to get away, she'd forgotten her gloves.

Christmas Eve morning. Early, the Carson house already alive with activity. Her nieces and nephews were little bundles of excited anticipation. Her brothers and sisters, their wives and husbands, harried by their children's antics, yet loving and indulgent at the same time.

The scent of sweet and spicy filled every room as Tula's mother cheerfully baked batch after batch of gingerbread for the coveted gift baskets she shared with her neighbors every year.

Normally, Tula would be in the kitchen, elbow deep in flour, helping. Or doing her best to entertain her siblings' hyperactive offspring. Instead, she'd slipped from her room, down the back stairs, and outside before anyone could commandeer her services as cook's helper *or* babysitter.

Tula needed time alone—a premium when her family was all together.

"I need to get over myself before I ruin the holiday with my long, suffering face."

Damn you, Fleet Sherman. Why did you have to be so wonderful? You didn't try to make me fall in love with you. You didn't mean to break my heart. Yet, here I am. Stuck with a mangled heart no longer my own.

Tula wished she had a solution. However, try as she might, she couldn't come up with a thing.

"There you are." Zoe trudged up the hill.

"What are you doing up here?" Tula looked the other woman up and down. Zoe's cheeks carried a healthy, rosy glow. And though her hair was slightly mussed from the quick climb, she was barely out of breath. Her coat, straight off the runway from New York. But on her feet? "Are those the rubber boots Mom bought at the hardware store to wear in the garden?"

Zoe never, *never* touched a pair of shoes unless they sported a designer label, let alone put them on her feet. Tula sobered.

"Has there been an accident? Who's hurt?"

"No accident. No injury." Zoe lifted her foot in the air, rotated her ankle from side to side and grimaced. "Surprisingly good traction. However, do my sense of fashion a favor? Next time you sneak off, take this with you."

Frowning, Tula took her phone from Zoe.

"Who would call me out here?"

"You never know." A twinkle in her eyes, Zoe blew Tula a kiss. "Bye."

Before Tula could protest, Zoe was on her way, back down the hill. And the phone rang. Still baffled, she checked the screen. Not a number she recognized.

"Hello," she answered, hesitant.

"Don't hang up."

"Fleet?" Tula's grip on the phone tightened. She longed to hear his voice. Why would she hang up?

"And don't say anything."

"Not even hello?"

"Just listen."

Listen? Tula's heartbeat was so loud, she couldn't hear herself think. How was she supposed to listen to…?

"Music."

Tula closed her eyes. Head tipped to one side, she kept the phone pressed to her ear, afraid to miss a single note. A simple arrangement. Just an acoustic guitar and Fleet's voice.

The song was something new. Yet, familiar. Different than any of Fleet's other compositions. Not sweet. Fleet didn't do sappy. Softer, but not mushy. The rhythm was romantic but never drifted into sentimental. And the words. Deeply emotional. Deeply personal. Tula's pulse skittered when she realized what he'd done.

Fleet Sherman had written a love song. A love song for her.

As the last note faded, the tears Tula held bottled inside since the night they said goodbye fell unchecked. She wanted Fleet. Here. Where she could see him. Touch him. Never let him go.

"Where are you? Tula's voice was surprisingly steady. "Why aren't you here?"

"Turn around."

Tula wanted to turn. More than anything. If only her body would cooperate.

"Never mind. I have you." From behind, Fleet's arms slid around Tula's waist. Warm. Strong. Steady. "I'll always have you. For as long you want me."

"Forever?"

Tula couldn't keep the hitch from her voice. The question was too important. Maybe the most important question she'd ever asked.

"Mmm." Fleet brushed his lips across her tear-soaked cheek. "How'd you guess?"

"Guess?" Tula leaned back, into his embrace. "What did I guess?"

"The name of the song." Fleet's warm breath caressed Tula's ear. "*Your* song."

Tula didn't think she had another tear to shed. She was wrong.

"*Forever?*"

Fleet nodded. Still snug in his arms, Tula turned. Over his dark hair, he wore a knit cap that framed his precious face. And, oh, what a face, she sighed happily. All hers. His smile. His gold-flecked eyes. Every gorgeous inch of him.

"You sealed your fate when you wrote me a song." Tula wound her arms around his neck. "You'll never get rid of me now."

"Promise?"

His brogue a little heavier than usual, an edge of vulnerability Tula had never seen before, entered his gaze. And she knew, if a single doubt had lingered, he was hers.

"When a Carson falls in love, we never waver. Never."

"I guess I need the words, Tula."

Of course, he did. Everybody did.

"I love you, Fleet. How could I not?" Tula touched his face. "You're a good man. Whether you know it or not."

"I want to be." Fleet kissed her forehead. "I'll try. Every day. For the rest of our lives."

"And I'll love you. Everyday. For the rest of our lives."

"I love you, Tula."

The kiss they shared was a beginning. Bold. Bright. Free of shadows.

"I almost forgot." Fleet laughed minutes later when they finally came up for air. With a flourish, he brought a bundle of roses from behind his back.

"Where were they?" Tula asked in wonder.

"I tucked them into the waistband of my jeans." He touched one drooping petal. "A bit worse for wear I'm afraid."

"They're perfect." She breathed in the heady fragrance. "Flowers in winter."

"Good title for a song." Fleet pulled her close. "Want to write it?

Happy beyond her wildest dreams, Tula nodded as he kissed the side of her neck.

"Together?"

Fleet raised Tula's hand to his lips, his hazel eyes flecked with gold.

"Forever."

EPILOGUE

"I WILL NEVER need to eat again," Fleet groaned. One arm around Tula's shoulders, he tipped his head back and breathed in the fresh mountain air.

"You didn't have to take a second piece of apple pie," Tula pointed out with a grin. "Or the two scoops of homemade ice cream."

"I couldn't say no. Your mother might think I didn't like her cooking."

No chance. Fleet had cleaned his plate. Roast beef. Potatoes. Gravy. Vegetables. Homemade bread. Between helpings, Fleet complimented the chef. And Nellie Carson beamed with pride.

"What about Mom's special Christmas morning cinnamon rolls?" Tula patted Fleet's impossibly flat stomach. "Should I tell Mom to give your share to somebody else?"

"Cinnamon rolls?" Fleet sighed with defeat. "I'll take a run before breakfast. And after. Maybe I should start now."

"Let's snuggle a bit first. If you don't mind."

"Now you're talking." Lips at Tula's temple, Fleet's arm around her tightened. "I think your family's great. However, the astounding number of them makes alone time difficult."

The porch swing swayed back and forth at a leisurely pace. Hours earlier, Tula sat in the exact same spot, certain she would never be anything but miserable for the rest of her life. Now? She was happy. Not a care in the world. Blue skies forever. Bone deep, happy.

"We're alone now."

"True." Fleet and Tula shared a brief, sigh-inducing kiss. "But for how long? Any second now, I expect your brother to plop himself down between us."

Smith had been slower to come around than the rest of Tula's family. Even her father—who didn't think any man was good enough for his daughters—had given Fleet a warm welcome. As soon as Smith realized how happy Tula was, he'd come around. She was certain.

"Zoe will keep Smith occupied."

"Good." Fleet placed his mouth close to Tula's ear. "I believe you owe me a limerick."

"Do I?" Tula laughed.

"When we first met, you said we'd have to know each other better before you could share one of your dirtier ditties."

"I remember."

"Well?"

"Come with me." Tula took Fleet's hand.

"Where are we going?" Fleet asked. Though he didn't hesitate to follow.

"You said you wanted to be alone. The barn is the only place where we won't be interrupted." Tula led the way across the driveway.

"Do you have in mind what I think?" Fleet sounded intrigued. And a bit leery. After all, he was a city boy, born and bred.

"The only witnesses out here are the cows. But don't worry, they're very circumspect."

Before Tula could open the barn door, Fleet placed a hand over hers.

"I'm all for getting naked." Fleet met her gaze. "We are getting naked?"

Eyes twinkling, Tula nodded.

"Isn't a barn in December a bit on the chilly side?"

Tula wasn't offended by his lack of enthusiasm. She didn't want to make love in an ice-cold box any more than Fleet.

"Climate controlled." A gift from Smith on their father's last birthday.

"Heat and privacy?" Fleet pulled open the door. "Sounds like heaven."

"Nope. Just Alabama." Grinning, Tula tumbled Fleet into a pile of loose hay. "How about a little foreplay? *There once was a man from Nantucket...*"

COMING IN 2018

◆ THE SISTERS QUARTET ◆

<u>FEBRUARY</u>
ONE OF THESE DAYS

<u>APRIL</u>
TWO OF A KIND

<u>JUNE</u>
THREE WISHES

<u>AUGUST</u>
FOUR SIMPLE WORDS

AFTER THE RAIN
(One Pass Away Book One)

PROLOGUE

LOGAN. LOGAN. LOGAN.

Logan Price closed his eyes, taking it all in.

"Hear that, kid?" Starting quarterback Gaige Benson slapped him on the back. "Two games under your belt and you're a star. Now let's go out there and add super to the front of it."

The announcer for the team set them in motion down the tunnel with his familiar introduction.

"And now, let's hear it for your division champion *SEATTLE KNIGHTS*."

The roar of the crowd. There was nothing like it. A packed stadium. Fans chanting his name. Few people would ever experience what it was like to take the field in a professional football game.

Logan Price had been working for this his entire life. He could still remember in exact detail the first game he ever saw. Too small to climb onto the stool in his father's bar by himself, his old man had lifted him onto the seat.

Stay and be quiet.

Not an easy order to follow for an active, inquisitive little boy. One look at the game and for once, Logan had no problem following his father's command. The old TV transported him to a foreign world filled with bright lights and shiny helmeted warriors. Logan didn't know what he was watching. He did know he wanted to be one of those men.

A Sunday afternoon in rural Oklahoma. *Lefty's Pub* was filled with after-church drinkers who figured they had done their duty to God and family. The rest of the day was their time. A beer. Or two. Or six. Cronies who understood a man's need to unwind before the start of another workweek.

And football.

If the Friday night high school game was their true religion, the Sunday afternoon games were a close second. As Oklahoma boys, they hated anything Texas. The men of Denville gathered every week to root for whichever team was playing the Dallas Cowboys.

No matter how the games ended. Whether the crowd was happy or disgruntled. It meant more drinking. Hours later, husbands, boyfriends, and sons would stumble out, pile into beat-up trucks, and weave their way home to frustrated wives, girlfriends, and mothers.

As he grew older, Logan's view changed. He moved from the stool to behind the bar. And he promised himself one thing. He would never become one of those men. He wouldn't spend the week at a job he hated. His home wouldn't be a semi-wide trailer filled with hand-me-down furniture and a wife to whom he couldn't face going home.

His Sundays were going to be spent playing football, not watching it.

"Ready to take down this vaunted Arizona defense?" Gaige yelled at him, butting helmets.

Vaunted. Good word, Logan thought. His QB liked to use what his granny called highfalutin talk. Must have been that Ivy League education. He knew that Gaige Benson didn't grow up with a silver spoon in his mouth. He came from the mean streets of Brooklyn. He had the scars to prove it.

Like Logan, Gaige had vowed to get out of the life into which he was born. In the process, he polished himself up like a new penny. He took advantage of his full-ride scholarship to Yale. He didn't spend all his time on the football field. Fancy vocabulary. Fancy clothes. Fancy women. They were all part of the package Gaige purposefully fashioned for himself.

Seventeen years after clawing his way out of the tenement that he grew up in, very little of that borough-rat remained. Until game time. No one was tougher than Gaige Benson. Three-time league MVP. Considered one of the best ever to play the game. No one stood in his way when he was playing the game. He had the scars to prove it.

"Gather round."

Knights head coach Harry Coleman gathered the team close. He had to yell over the crowd, but he had the voice to do it. Booming was putting it mildly. The first time Logan heard it, he stood right beside the man. The ringing in his ears didn't go away for three days.

"Divisional game. If I have to say any more than that, you shouldn't be out here. Go kick some ass."

The defense took the field to start the game. Arizona had a rookie quarterback drafted in the second round from a small college in the Midwest. The only reason he was out there was because the regular starter suffered a concussion in last week's game and the regular backup had food poisoning. Thrown into action at the last minute, Logan swore he could see the guy's hands shaking before he took the first snap. When the ball went sailing between his legs, Logan shook his head.

The moment was too big for some people. For Logan, it wasn't big enough. He aimed for the biggest stage of all. The Super Bowl. It wasn't a matter of *if* he would get there, but when.

"Three and out." Gaige grinned, pulling on his helmet. "Come on, kid. Let's go show them how it's done."

Logan ran onto the field. *Kid.* He shook his head, grinning. From the first day of training camp, Gaige had hung that moniker on him. Ironic since he was almost twenty-five, a good two years older than most of the other rookies. However, he supposed when someone had been in the league as long as Gaige, all the new guys seemed like kids.

"We're starting on the ground," Gaige instructed them in the huddle. "Sweep out left. Basic. Got it?"

Lining up as he had a thousand other times, Logan checked the defense. He knew he was fast. One of the fastest in the game. What set him apart was his anticipation. He had the uncanny ability to read the guy covering him. He knew when to fake left or when to fake right. Stutter step or flat out, in your face, catch me if you can.

His speed got him out of Denville, Oklahoma. His brains and determination got him to the NFL.

The sounds of the game were as familiar to Logan as the back of his own hand. The call from scrimmage. Each quarterback had his own unique cadence. Gaige was a master of mixing his up. Study him all you want. Good luck figuring it out. His teammates knew. A signal just before they broke the huddle.

Pay attention, you were golden. Slack off even once? Gaige could ream a guy out with the best of them. And he had no problem doing it in the middle of the game.

An entire YouTube channel had been devoted to Gaige and his rants. They were as legendary as the man himself. With a ball in his hand, he was cool as ice. The rest of the time, watch out.

No one would ever accuse Logan of lacking focus. Today was no exception. They were driving down the field. First and ten from the Arizona twenty-yard line. He already had three carries of thirty-five yards. It was going to be a good day.

"Ready to take it in?" Gaige asked.

"Always."

"Then show them what you've got."

A quick snap later, Gaige handed the ball to Logan. The offensive line created a seam. Not a big one. Just big enough. Using the push of his powerful legs, Logan surged through. One more step. They wouldn't catch him. No one could.

Like everything connected with the game, Logan heard the snap of the bone with total clarity. The agony that surged through his body was so intense he almost passed out. In the next few minutes, he was going to wish he had.

"Get back." Logan heard Gaige through the haze of pain. "Goddamn it. Move the hell off."

The three-hundred-and-fifty-pound linebacker didn't get off by standing. He rolled. Crushing Logan's broken leg as he went. He would never know if the move had been deliberate. Now, it was the last thing on his mind. He only cared about two things. How bad was the injury and when would he be able to play again.

"Hold on, kid." Gaige took his hand. "They're bringing the stretcher."

The team doctor checked his eyes. Logan knew he was asked some questions. What they were and how he answered, he would never remember. By the time they carted him off the field, Logan knew the break was bad.

"Gaige." Logan reached for him.

"I'm here, kid."

"Is it over?"

"The game?" Gaige walked with him, his head bent toward Logan. "No. But I promise we're going to win the bastard."

They loaded him onto the open cart. They had him secured and the vehicle rolled away before Logan had his answer. He wasn't wondering about the game. It was his career.

To no one in particular, he whispered the question again.

"Is it over?"

CHAPTER ONE

LOGAN SAT UP in bed, his body covered with a fine coating of sweat.

He glanced at the clock. Three in the fucking morning. On the one night he managed to get to bed at a reasonable hour, he was plagued by the nightmare that had haunted his dreams for the past two years.

Running his hand through his long, damp hair, Logan fell back onto the mattress. His sheets were as wet as he was. With a grimace, he rolled onto the floor. Flexing his stiff knee, he stripped the bed, tossing everything onto a pile of dirty clothes he planned on taking to the laundromat on his day off.

There was an alternative. He could always take Linda Sue Hemmings up on her offer. She would do his laundry anytime. Payment. On-call stud service whenever her husband Darryl was out of town on business. As much as Logan hated folding socks, he decided the price was too high. He had lost a lot in the last few years. He still held onto his dignity. Just barely.

Still groggy, Logan shuffled to the bathroom. Flipping on the light, he grimaced at what the mirror reflected.

Too many late nights followed by not enough sleep. As patterns went, it wasn't a healthy one. Perpetually bloodshot eyes.

Dark circles on his dark circles. He needed a haircut. Logan ran his hand over his face. Even more, he needed a shave.

He had to hand it to himself. When he let himself go, he went all the way. All he had to do was stop showering. If he wasn't worried about driving the customers away with his smell, he might have considered it.

The old plumbing rattled with protest when he turned on the faucet. It wasn't a bad place. There were worse. Logan splashed some cold water on his face. He didn't bother with a towel. It would dry soon enough on its own.

He had two choices.

Toss and turn for a couple of hours on the unmade bed – he really needed to get more than one set of sheets.

Or lose himself with an old friend.

Sleep wasn't coming which made the choice an easy one.

Logan pulled on a pair of old shorts, a faded t-shirt and sweatshirt that was too ratty to be called anything as fashionable as a hoodie. After lacing up his sneakers, he hit the road. When he was a kid, he ran for the fun of it. In high school and college, it strengthened his legs and improved his stamina. Now, the only thing it accomplished was getting him a reputation as that half-crazy Price boy. Running the deserted streets at all hours? Maybe his head had been permanently injured along with his leg.

Logan jogged past *Lefty's Pub*. The place where he spent most evenings tending bar. The day he left for college he swore to anyone who would listen that he had served his last beer. Eight years later, here he was, washing glasses and putting up with not so subtle jabs about how the mighty had fallen.

Coming back to Denville was more of an adjustment than Logan anticipated. He expected the cracks about his failed NFL career. Any kind of success tended to breed a certain amount of jealousy and resentment. There were those who reveled in his injury.

Logan Price always thought too much of himself. Denville wasn't good enough for the high school's star running back. He forgot all about us when he made it big.

The sound of his feet pounding on the unpaved side street couldn't keep the usual thoughts from creeping back. Some of what those people said was true. He had been full of himself. At seventeen, one wasn't written up in national magazines without it going to his head.

Logan never tried to hide his plans. A full-ride scholarship to the college of his choice. Then the pros. MVP awards. Super Bowl rings. The cocky attitude of a teenager wasn't any easier to take than if he had been an adult. Most of Denville embraced their golden boy.

GRAB YOUR COPY TODAY

http://amzn.to/2lUqmqY

AFTER ALL THESE YEARS
(One Pass Away Book Two)

PROLOGUE

SEAN McBRIDE WOKE up with a smile on his face. It happened a lot lately. And he thoroughly approved.

He stretched his long, athletic body. Some mornings every inch of him ached. Such was the life of a professional football player. Everything was about preparing for the game. Focus. Concentration. The goal was to be ready for game day.

He had to hold it together for sixty minutes. Pull out a win any way possible. Sacrifice his body to the football Gods and pray he walked away healthy enough to do it all again next week.

Sean dreaded the day after the game. The adrenaline had long ago worn off and he felt all of his thirty years. There were degrees of bad. Sometimes he shuffled to the shower, the aches and pains palpable, but mercifully bearable.

Then there were the bad days. After a day of three-hundred-pound defensive backs using him as their own personal punching bag, he didn't get out of bed—he crawled.

Bruised from top to bottom, his joints creaked and his muscles protested like screeching banshees. Those were the times he wondered why he did it. He could have been a doctor. Or a lawyer. He could have taken his father's advice and gone into the family business. No seventeen-year-old with dreams of glory in the NFL wanted to think about becoming a butcher. But damn. Cutting meat sounded good on those mornings.

This was a good Monday. His body felt lithe—limber. The bruises were there. That was part of his life. However, yesterday had been one of those rare games when every moment fell into place. From the kickoff to the final whistle, the outcome of the game was never in question.

Sean caught every ball thrown his way. He evaded the defense. Fast as the wind. Three touchdowns. One hundred and eighty-two total yards. A damn good day for any wide receiver. He would have had more if Coach Coleman hadn't taken him out of the game in the fourth quarter. With a big lead, there was no reason to risk injury when he wasn't needed.

The after-game celebration moved from the locker room to one of the team's favorite hangouts. Naturally the atmosphere was raucous. Cautiously so.

The Knights were having a stellar season. Ten wins, two losses. Sean and his friends had enough games under their belts to understand how quickly that could turn. Injuries tended to come in bunches. So far, they were healthy. However, that was bound to change. The hope was to get to the playoffs with all their major players on the roster.

After the game, they had a few drinks. Three was Sean's limit these days. A few years ago it was a different story. He would have closed the place down after a win. He and his bed partner of the moment would have moved on to someone's apartment, partying until dawn before going back to her place and fucking like demented rabbits. Then he would go home alone and catch a few hours sleep until it was time to grab a quick shower before heading to the Knights' headquarters to review film from the game.

Those days were over. Sean wasn't a kid anymore, high on his own press clippings and more testosterone than brains. Not that he had settled down completely. He could still party with the best of them. However, he chose his moments—ones that never took place during the season.

Women were another matter. Sean liked sex. Always had. If there were a God, he always would. While his bed partners weren't as varied, they were almost as frequent.

Sean knew players who abstained a few days before the game, saving their *juice*. He wasn't one of them. Sean had plenty of juice, thank you very much. Sex was necessary for a happy and healthy mind. For *his* happy and healthy mind.

A big plus to having sex at night was sex the next morning. It was one of his favorite things. A partner, warm and willing.

The perfect way to start the day.

Speaking of which. Smiling, Sean turned over. His hand reached out, expecting to find a soft, sweet woman. Instead, he found cold sheets. Sitting up, he looked around the room. Like the bed, empty. The bathroom door was open and the light off.

Not bothering to cover up, Sean jumped out of bed. Buck naked, he searched the house. She wasn't in the kitchen. Why would she be? She didn't cook, not even coffee. She was on a first-name basis with half the baristas in Seattle.

Was that it? Would she be back soon with two cups of steaming black caffeine and his favorite muffins? Sean was talking himself into that scenario when he saw the note.

He picked up the paper that had been propped against the lamp by the front door.

Sean.

Thank you for the past few weeks. After years of building it up in my mind, I was worried that it couldn't live up to my expectations. I should have known better. It was everything I had hoped for—and more.

We didn't make any promises. No strings were attached that need to be broken. After all these years, you can finally breathe easy. It's over. We are now friends without the expectation of benefits.

When we see each other, it will be as if it, we, never happened.

Sean read the note. Then read it again.

What the fuck? What was in those drinks?

Sean searched his memory for some kind of clue. The bar. His teammates. Then she was there. They laughed. Everything was smooth and easy. They seemed to be developing a rhythm. In his mind, they were together. Not a man and a woman—a couple.

It sounded good to him. He would have sworn she felt the same. He didn't want another woman. He wanted her. In his arms. In his life.

No expectations? Hell. He woke up with plenty of them, only to find out he was alone. Alone in bed. Alone. Period.

Sean scrubbed a hand over his face. He remembered the way she tasted. The way she melted into his arms. The curves of her luscious body pressed against his. Her sighs. His belief he would never get enough of her.

Crumpling the note into a ball, Sean tossed it across the room. Suddenly he felt every ache. His legs felt like lead. Slowly, he shuffled toward the bathroom. He needed a shower. Long and hot. Determined not to look at the bed, Sean's peripheral vision wouldn't let him off the hook that easily. It captured everything. The rumpled sheet. The pillow still holding the imprint of her head. A slash of red on the floor.

Frowning, Sean picked up the scrap of silk. So small he wondered why she had bothered. The image of her standing in nothing but her heels and the panties popped into his head. Unconsciously, his body tightened with desire.

Right, that was why.

Sean ran the smooth material over his cheek, feeling it catch on his morning stubble. He breathed deeply. He smelled vanilla and spice. Her essence. He would never forget it. As long as he lived, he would be able to close his eyes and conjure up her scent. Her taste.

His eyes popped open. *Friends? Nothing more? Bullshit*!

Keeping the panties in his hand, Sean headed for the shower. This wasn't over. Not by a long shot. It was just the beginning.

YOUR COPY IS WAITING ONE CLICK AWAY

http://amzn.to/2nmMFma

AFTER THE FIRE
(One Pass Away Book Three)

PROLOGUE

SHE HAD ONCE asked him if he believed in a higher power.

God? Buddha? Fairies dancing around a blazing fire late at night? Something. Anything bigger than us.

Gaige Benson hadn't known what to say. Not then. But as he stood in the empty open-air stadium—the stars lighting the evening sky—he knew the answer.

Football was his religion. The field he played on and the building surrounding it, his cathedral. If a higher power had a hand in it, then his answer was yes.

He believed.

Walking to the center of the field, Gaige took it all in. He found football at the age of thirteen. A boy who saw his future mapped out. Working in a factory. Drinking away his salary. Divorce. Doling out child support without maintaining a relationship with his children. A weekend father, who half the time didn't bother to show up.

The first time Gaige picked up a football, he felt a connection. The first time he threw it, it wobbled with the grace of a drunk leaving his favorite watering hole on a Saturday night. But it didn't matter. He threw the ball again. And again. Until he taught himself to make it spin in a perfect spiral.

At the time, Gaige didn't know his talent could be useful. Where he came from, Brooklyn kids didn't dream of bigger or better. Most of them didn't dream at all. Gaige was no different.

One day he was passing a playground when a football landed at his feet. The boys on the field yelled for him to toss it back. Without thinking, Gaige sent it sailing, a perfect strike. Then kept walking. He was wary of the man who ran after him. Strangers were the enemy—according to his father. They either wanted money or accused you of something you hadn't done.

Gaige took everything his father said with a big grain of salt. Don Benson didn't have a dime to his name. Why would anyone expect to get money from him? And if a man accused his father of something, chances were he was guilty.

But Gaige was a cautious boy. He fought when necessary and ran when he had no choice. The man trying to get his attention was big. His dark complexion didn't worry Gaige. In his experience, a man was either good or bad. The color of his skin had nothing to do with it.

It turned out that this man wasn't simply good. He was the best thing that ever happened to Gaige.

Terrance Aldridge coached the local Pop Warner football team. A boy with an arm like Gaige's shouldn't let his talent go to waste. Gaige listened. Play football? On a field? With other boys? Was such a thing possible? He didn't know if it were a scam—nor did he care. If there were the slightest chance, he would take it.

The only obstacle was getting a parent's permission. Terrance gave him the papers to be signed, telling Gaige to have his folks call him if they had any questions. Gaige didn't laugh aloud, but he wanted to. His mother never asked questions. Unless they were directed at his father. Wynona Benson hadn't made a move in fifteen years unless she received permission first.

His father was another matter. His word was law. Don Benson could do no wrong. If he drank too much and staggered home two days late, it was his right. If he backhanded his wife—just because—whose business was it? He earned the money. He made the rules. End of discussion.

Gaige hadn't asked his father because he knew what the answer would be. No! Not because he thought there was anything wrong with football. He watched it every Sunday—after laying down a bet that he never won. No, he wouldn't let Gaige play because he was a mean bastard who wanted everyone to be as miserable as he was.

Gaige got around it easily enough. He forged his father's signature. It wasn't the first time and it wouldn't be the last. There was no reason to think anyone would find out. His parents didn't care how he spent his days as long as the police didn't come knocking on the door.

He could steal. Lie. Cheat. Hell, his father wouldn't bat an eye at murder. *Do what you want as long as you don't get caught.* The mantra at the Benson house.

Gaige had no intention of his father finding out. He tried out for the team and made it. The money for equipment was another matter. Gaige didn't steal. Or cheat. Lying was a necessary evil. He would have done almost anything to play but it looked like his first and only dream would die before it had a chance.

Luckily, Terrance was able to dip into a discretionary fund to help boys like Gaige. It rankled to take charity. Especially when the other boys on the team had families to pay their way.

"Don't let it stop you, Gaige," Terrance told him. "Remember. And one day, when you have the means, pay it forward, son."

Twenty-five years later, Gaige hadn't forgotten that kindness and generosity. When he saw someone in need, he did something about it. Over the years, the *Gaige Benson Foundation* paid out millions of dollars to charities and individuals. He had filled the board with people he trusted and could count on to distribute the funds judiciously and without prejudice. The first man he had recruited was the man to whom Gaige owed everything—Terrance Aldridge. Friend. Father figure. Teacher.

"Hey, Gaige." Logan Price called out from high in the stands. "You coming? The guys are waiting to go to dinner."

"Five minutes."

Closing his eyes, Gaige breathed in the air. February in Texas. Tomorrow he would play in his first—and last Super Bowl. Win or lose, he was hanging up his cleats. He was thirty-eight years old. He had more money than he would ever need. He had won every award from Rookie of the Year to league MVP—four times.

This season he put everything on the line to get here—including the possibility that he had lost the only woman he had ever loved.

Gaige Benson was known for his razor-sharp focus. Any distractions off the field were left there as soon as the first whistle blew. It wouldn't be any different tomorrow. Nothing would get in the way.

His gaze drifted to the section where she would be sitting. If she showed up. Gaige planned on going out a winner. But what about the day after? Or the day after that? His future stretched out in front of him. He had plans in place. There were hundreds of options for him to consider.

Do you believe in a higher power?

Her voice and that question had haunted Gaige for almost sixteen years. If there were a God, he prayed the woman he loved

167

would find it in her heart to forgive him. He had a lot of years left. He didn't want to spend them alone.

In his lifetime, Gaige Benson had dreamt of only two things. Playing football. And loving Violet Reed.

YOUR COPY IS WAITING ONE CLICK AWAY

http://amzn.to/2mTO31R

DREAMING WITH A BROKEN HEART
(Hollywood Legends Book One

PROLOGUE

THE ROOM WAS dark. Too dark for Garrett's liking. A little stuffy, a slight antiseptic smell with an overlay of sex. That's what you got from a cheap motel and furtive lovemaking. Odors and memories you'd just as soon forget.

The sounds from behind the closed bathroom door indicated his partner was trying to remove all traces of their recent activities. It shouldn't hurt. This wasn't the first time, and damn his weak resolve, it wouldn't be the last.

If he smoked, he would have something to do with his hands. Watching his father struggle with lung cancer put the fear of God in him and his brothers at an early age. All four of them had their vices; smoking wasn't one of them.

Get up. Get dressed. For once, be the first to leave. Even if he could find the balls to walk out on her, he couldn't leave her alone at this time of night. In this part of town.

God, it was like a furnace in here. Despite having the AC wall unit on high, Garrett knew it must be hotter in here than outside. The sheet riding low on his hips was too much. Damn modesty.

The room was too dark to see anything; if she didn't like seeing his naked body, she could turn away. Garrett whipped off the coarse cotton material at the same moment the bathroom door opened.

"You don't have to go," Garrett said to the shadowed figure.

"Yes, I do."

She always made sure the light was off. Her silhouette showed a tall woman, thin. Too thin. Even by L.A. standards. She was gaining weight — slowly. Garrett could attest to that. He knew it was a struggle. One she fought every day.

Garrett felt the anger drain from his body — his heart melt. Her demands were not capricious whims. They weren't her attempt to gain the upper hand. Her goal was not to manipulate. She had her reasons. They were real. Legitimate.

"It's still early."

Garrett kept his voice low and even. Shouting didn't help. She never fought back. Retreat. That was her coping mechanism. The last time he blew up it was two weeks before she would take his calls.

"I..." she cleared her voice. "His flight gets in at midnight."

"Don't be there."

"You know how he gets."

Garrett knew all right. She was devoted to a man who treated her like crap, forgot her existence ninety percent of the time, yet expected her to be there when he decided to come home. His fists clenched the mattress. It was the only thing preventing him from grabbing her, begging her to stay. *For once, pick me.*

"I don't know when I can see you again."

I don't know if I ever want to see you again. Garrett thought the words. He would never verbalize them. She was his drug of choice. Weeks passed. The need for her grew. Outwardly, his life looked smooth as glass. Inside, the itch grew.

Garrett became an expert at compartmentalizing. His work never suffered. His family never suspected. No one had the slightest clue about what was raging inside of him. *She* knew. Because she shared his unbreakable habit. Enablers. That's what they were. It was sick. Sometimes, like tonight, he hated himself. He wished he could hate her. Then, maybe, he could walk away.

"I'll be out of town for the next month."

Garrett wished he could see her face. Was she sorry he'd be gone? Relieved? Would she miss him half as much as he was going to miss her?

"Take care."

Garrett waited a second, letting the motel room door close behind her. Jumping up, rushing to the window, he pulled back the thin, dingy curtain. He never walked her to the taxi. Even the minutest chance of them being seen was too much.

The ritual of watching until she was safely inside the vehicle, seat belt on, doors locked, was something he never ignored.

Nothing bad would happen to her when he was around. It was when he wasn't there that trouble found her. One more frustration. It wasn't his place to protect her. Knowing that drove him crazy.

Garrett grabbed his jeans from a nearby chair, pulling them on. Unlike her, he wouldn't clean up before he left. He would carry the smell of her with him — let it fill the interior of his car. Tomorrow he would pretend it was still there.

Damn it. Enough. He deserved more than this. They both did. One month. When he got back, one way or another, things were going to change.

CHAPTER ONE

HOLLYWOOD. DREAMS FULFILLED. Dreams crushed. It happened every day. Wide-eyed kids still came hoping to be a star. More often than not, they went back home — a nobody. Iowa, Nebraska, Texas, Georgia. Insert state here. Small town, big city. It didn't matter. The movie industry seemed vast from the outside. In truth, it was the most insular of worlds. Making it took determination, perseverance, and a whole lot of luck. Talent was so far down the list it wasn't funny.

Connections. That was what got you through the door. If you had a recognizable name, the door swung wide, the smiles welcoming. If you couldn't pull your weight once you were inside, no one hesitated to kick you out. That famous name only got you so far. The rest was on your shoulders.

Sink or swim. No life preservers were thrown your way. If anything, you were fitted with cement shoes. The only thing this town loved more than a winner was the child of a Hollywood legend falling flat on his face.

Garrett Landis felt the weight of those expectations every time he stepped on a movie set. His father set the bar so high none of his sons was expected to reach his lofty heights. The fact that all four seemed well on their way to not only matching Caleb Landis' achievements, but surpassing them, caused quite a stir.

Resentment simmered under the surface of hearty backslapping and insincere ass kissing. Their father taught his boys many things. In this business, never turn your back on friend or foe. Treat everyone with respect, from the lowliest crew member to the head of the studio. The most important thing? In this business, trust no one — except brothers. Eight years after making his first low-budget independent film, Garrett followed those rules without question. The Gospel according to Caleb Landis. His father's words were his bible. His brothers were his rock.

Wyatt, the oldest, followed directly in their father's footsteps. He was a hard-ass, bottom-line producer. Nathaniel, Garrett's fraternal twin, was the daredevil of the bunch. He was the most in-demand stuntman in Hollywood. Baby brother Colton was blessed with movie star looks. His charisma leaped off the screen, pulling in even the most cynical audience member. Or so one critic wrote after seeing Colt's first movie. Individually, each Landis brother was formidable. Together, they dominated almost every branch of the industry.

"How can we be behind schedule when we haven't shot a single frame?"

"Welcome to the glamorous world of moviemaking."

Garrett grinned when he answered his assistant director, Hamish Floyd. This was their fourth collaboration. The first two made a nice profit. Number three broke box office records.

Expectations for *Exile* went through the roof the second Garrett's name became attached. With Wyatt behind the scenes, the movie's success was practically guaranteed.

Garrett didn't believe in sure things. He worked hard on every project, no matter the size. Bigger budget, more potential headaches. That included a prima donna leading lady who couldn't get her ass on set at the designated hour. Garrett refused to start leaking money on day one.

"You want me to coax America's sweetheart of the week out of her trailer?"

"You'd never get past her PA," Garrett told Hamish. "Lynne Cornish thinks one hit movie and a few magazine covers give her the right to make her own rules. She's going to find out on this movie set, there is only one set of rules — mine."

"She has a contract."

"Wyatt's standard contract. She signed it. Her mistake if her lawyers didn't read the fine print."

Contracts were fluid. *Before* they were finalized. Each actor, depending on their box office leverage, could get their people to make demands, tweak the perks. The basics were non-negotiable. Under no circumstance, barring personal injury, a death in the family, or a genuine nervous breakdown, was an actor allowed to delay production. Once, you were warned. Twice, bye-bye. As far as Garrett's big brother was concerned, potential loss of a lead actor was the reason they paid huge insurance premiums. It hadn't happened to Garrett. Not yet. There was always a first time.

Tim Bodine, Lynne Cornish's PA, waylaid Garrett before he was halfway to her trailer.

"Lynne isn't feeling well."

"She was fine an hour ago."

When she was flirting with every man on the set. Apparently, Ms. Cornish could drag herself to any early breakfast if adoring men were present. She found out quickly that Garrett wasn't among them. Whether her sudden *illness* was a result of a hurt ego or plain laziness, he didn't give a damn. Starting right now, Lynne Cornish needed to know who was boss.

"Does she need a doctor?"

"Nooo." Tim drew out the word.

The PA's lack of concern only ratcheted up Garrett's annoyance.

"Five minutes."

"What?" Tim yelled at Garrett's retreating figure. When there was no response, the man hurried to catch up. "She can't make it in five minutes. Lynne doesn't think today will work for her. At all."

Garrett rounded on the smaller man. He topped him by at least eight inches. Tim was slight, Garrett muscular. Yet that wasn't what had the PA stepping back several feet. It was the look in Garrett's steely eyes.

This man exuded confidence. Strength, both physical and psychological, radiated from his core. You didn't mess with Garrett Landis. Not if you had half a brain.

"She was looking a little better when I left her trailer," Tim said, clearing his throat. "She wanted to speak with you. *Privately.*"

Well, shit. Garrett didn't see that coming. Lynne made it clear, early on –she was interested. He made it equally clear he wasn't. End of story. They would have a friendly, professional relationship. Finding out his beautiful leading lady was angling for more didn't hold the thrill it once had. It made Garrett... tired. His personal life was full of enough turmoil — he didn't need the added drama of an on-set romance.

"I don't have the time, or inclination, Tim."

To Garrett's surprise, the PA blushed. In Hollywood, that ability was knocked out of a person fast.

"I can't guarantee anything."

"Then Lynne will be out of a job. How long do you think you'll last after that?"

Tim Bodine looked like a smart man. One capable of cajoling his uncooperative employer. Garrett didn't care what it took to get his star in front of the camera as long as it happened. Immediately.

"Five minutes?" Tim asked, a little panicked.

"I'll give you ten."

Garrett wondered if it was too late to get out of feature films. Animation. That sounded good. No location shoots. Voice-over actors happy to skip wardrobe fittings and hours in the makeup chair. A little direction on his part. Mostly setting the scene. One or two takes. Right now, it sounded like heaven.

"What's the word?" Hamish asked him.

"Bitch?"

"Any chance she'll be joining us in the near future?"

"Your guess is as good as mine."

Garrett looked around. They were ready to go. Cameras primed, leading man looking as impatient as Garrett felt. At least he'd lucked out with Paul McNally. He was a professional through and through. No power plays. No outlandish demands. There was no propositioning the director. Paul's first job was a small part in a Caleb Landis production. He was a great actor. More importantly, he was a friend. Garrett felt lucky to work with him.

"Once again, you've lived up to your reputation," Hamish said with admiration. "You really are a miracle worker."

Garrett looked over his shoulder. Lynne Cornish. In full costume and makeup. A little pouty. He could work with that. It complimented the scene.

"Tell them five."

"We're shooting in five minutes, people," Hamish called out Garrett's directions. "Pee now or forever hold it."

Garrett moved over to camera A, checking the shot. Perfect. This was his world. He knew what he was doing. No one questioned his authority or failed to jump at his command. Unlike his personal life, his professional life stayed on a clear path.

GRAB YOUR COPY NOW

www.ingramcontent.com/pod-product-compliance
Lightning Source LLC
Chambersburg PA
CBHW060815120626
46557CB00001B/229